RAVAGE MC BOUND SERIES BOOK THREE

BOUND
BY *Vengeance*
RYAN MICHELE

1st edition published: September 14, 2017
Editing by: C&D Editing
Proofread: Silla Webb
Cover Design by: Cassy Roop at Pink Ink Designs
Photography by: Wander Aguiar
Models: Jonny James and Desiree Crossmann

TABLE OF CONTENTS

Prologue

Chapter One

Chapter Two

Chapter Three

Chapter Four

Chapter Five

Chapter Six

Chapter Seven

Chapter Eight

Chapter Nine

Chapter Ten

Chapter Eleven

Chapter Twelve

Chapter Thirteen

Chapter Fourteen

Chapter Fifteen

Chapter Sixteen

Chapter Seventeen

Chapter Eighteen

Chapter Nineteen

Chapter Twenty

Chapter Twenty-One

Chapter Twenty-Two

Chapter Twenty-Three

Chapter Twenty-Four

Chapter Twenty-Five

Chapter Twenty-Six

Chapter Twenty-Seven

Epilogue

Bonus—Austyn

About the Author

Acknowledgements

Other Works by Ryan Michele

PROLOGUE

Austyn

The gun is steady in my hand, the weight of it not giving me a bit of comfort. The cold of the metal, the unforgiveness of its mold, it matches the way I feel inside. Hardened steel, molded and made by the hands of men, the firearm gives me no fear. It only feeds the burning need for retribution in my soul.

Aiming it at him, thoughts of how I got to this place rush through me. The choices that were stripped, the consequences of actions and life that were altered and changed forever. All of it weighs heavily on me, but my strong shoulders bear it.

Being a warrior is in my blood, carried through me from my parents. Eye for an eye is our motto. They would expect nothing less from me.

The blood pumping through my veins was once a life source. Now, my sole focus and the fury that courses through me is fueled by vengeance with every beat of my heart.

He looks up at me, eyes blank.

"Bye, Ryker."

Without a second thought or a moment of hesitation, I pull the trigger.

CHAPTER ONE

Austyn

"Oh, Austyn." Lexa, my former and hopefully current boss, tightly wraps her arms around me, tipping my body from left to right in excitement. Her short, spiked hair pokes me as she leans in.

She's always stylish, staying with the latest trends and colors. Currently, the tips are a vibrant pink, but will surely change next week.

"Hi, Lexa."

It's been three and a half months since I stepped foot into Do or Dye Salon. Truthfully, I didn't know how Lexa would react to me coming in without any notice. When I left, it was by phone, not wanting to be out in the world, unable to handle people. She was worried, and I knew she cared because she showed it every day I worked here for the past year and a half. Life was hard, and it took me away for a while.

This salon is my third home, right after my parents' house and the Ravage MC clubhouse. They always say that home is where you hang your hat, but for me, it's where I have people around me that I care about.

Lexa pulls away, yet still holding on to me as she looks me up and down. Shying away isn't an option. There are no physical markings anyone can see. It's what's on the inside that can be scary. Good thing that is well-hidden.

It's my secret, my scars. No one can bear the burden but me.

There is a piece of me that started small and dark, but now it has grown to cover every inch of my soul. Seeking equality and vengeance, the woman at the core of who I am is marked, stained, covered in red.

Once life was my oyster, or whatever the fuck the saying is. Once I was carefree. Once I was open to life, love, and anything that came my way. Now I have a fortress around myself. It's a good thing no one can penetrate those walls. I'll make damn sure that doesn't happen.

"Tell me you're coming back. We've had requests for you up and down, and I need you!"

This is music to my ears. Not only do I need to work, I need a paycheck. Life continues, even when you don't want it to. It's a lesson I learned the hard way, and money is survival at its finest.

"If you'll have me."

Her smile lifts so high I swear her ears move with a wiggle. "Yes! Can you start now? I didn't put anyone in your chair and haven't touched a thing."

This surprises me. Do or Dye Salon is small with only five chairs that are normally filled all the time. It's only open for a specific few hours, and by appointment only. We take walk-ins, but they understand they could possibly be waiting all day before a spot opens. The place is constantly packed with people wanting a fresh look or a root touch-up. The fact that Lexa kept my spot after the phone call and over the months shows her loyalty and makes me love her even more.

I scrunch my face up. "Maybe I should clean my station first?"

She waves her hand in front of her like she's shooing away a fly. "Nonsense. I've kept it clean. And no one has cut hair there. Once word gets out that you're back, the place will be hopping!"

"It's not already?" When I came in, three of the five chairs were filled.

"Not nearly enough since you left. Now that you're back, it'll be rocking!" She steps away and goes to her computer, typing in some keys. "There, you're all ready to start. You can do walk-ins until people know you're back, but let me tell you, it won't take but a day for the news to get out and the phone to light up. I'm going to have to warn Kari so she can expect the phone and the desk to be backed up."

This is exactly what I needed.

"I'm sure Emery will come in. She's been buggin' the hell out of me to do her hair. I told her I'd do it at my mom's, but she says it isn't the same."

Lexa's face lights up with glee. If there's anything she loves, it's when people talk about her shop and make it known that she's the best in town.

"Call her up. Get her in here. This is great!"

Great is right. This endeavor went so much better than I envisioned. I thought she wouldn't want me back after leaving her high and dry on a whim. Luckily, she still likes me. I wonder, though, how long it's going to take before she asks me where I was and why I didn't come to work. That isn't a conversation I'm looking forward to.

An hour later, the bell over the door rings and Emery, my best friend and cousin, strolls into the place, looking like she's won the

11

lottery.

She has the most beautiful hair. It's long, almost down to her butt, straight, and so silky smooth it makes those television commercials for shampoo look like child's play. She always insists on adding highlights, but I think she's nuts. Her hair doesn't need them because she has natural ones that people here would love to have. I do it for her, anyway.

"I'm so excited!" She comes over, giving me a hug before setting her purse down on the small table against the window. The shop is set up a bit strange, but considering the way the building is, there isn't much of a choice.

When you walk in the front door, there is a small reception desk to the left, then the five stations where the stylists work are to the right. Five black chairs with cabinets and large mirrors on the walls. Next to those are the four sinks for shampooing, and next to that are the hair dryers. On the opposite wall is the bathroom and places to sit and hang coats. It's long instead of wide. Small, simple.

What I like best about it is it's painted a vibrant purple on three of the walls and a cream on the other. Lexa has it decorated with stylish paintings. It's a very comfortable place to work.

"Me too. What do you want to do?"

As Emery plops down in my chair, I drape my leopard print cape over her body and snap it at the nape.

"The usual. I need a trim too. What do you think of layers?"

I grab the brush and begin to glide it down her hair. Needing to put her up some, I then give the chair a pump with my foot to raise her before continuing my task. "If that's what you want, we can totally do it. You'd be adorable."

Her eyes narrow. "Adorable? You seriously just used the word adorable with me?"

A chuckle escapes. "Yep. Adorably cute."

She reaches out and smacks me on the arm playfully. "That's not funny, missy."

When we were younger, she'd let me "practice" on her, and I use that term loosely. No matter what I did to her hair—and one time I cut a huge chunk out of it—it was always *adorable*. It got to the point where she told me, if I used that word again, she wouldn't allow me to do her hair anymore. So, I moved to the word cute. Then that word got banned.

"Sure it was. Let's do this."

"Let's."

Being behind the chair, holding the foil in my hand and smelling the lifter in my nostrils, it all feels normal. Right. I've missed this. I needed this. My life is getting back on track.

"Have you heard from Micah since you moved back home?" I ask.

Emery moved back to Sumner when her mother was diagnosed with cancer. She's been going to community college and taking some online classes. Micah, Tug and Blaze's kid, has been her childhood crush forever. They even went away to the same school.

"Hell no," she growls, piquing my interest.

I roll her hair in a foil before pressing it to her head, using the metal end of the comb to fold the edges. "What does that mean?"

"He had a girlfriend and decided to bring her with him when he came to see me. Me, I thought it would be just him and me. Got dressed up and all that shit. Anyway, I ended up faking being sick so I could go home."

"What a dick."

She looks at me in the mirror, eyes brimming with unshed tears. "She was a brunette and really, really pretty. I probably would have liked her if she wasn't hanging on Micah's arm. But whatever. That's over. He's there, I'm here, and he doesn't want anything to do with the club, so I don't have to worry about him coming home."

"What if he does come home?" I ask, parting another strand of hair.

"He won't." The confidence in her voice has me thinking she may be right. If she's wrong, it could go really bad really fast.

"Are we still on to get that place together?" she asks, changing the subject as she stares down at her phone, no doubt on social media. The woman does statuses and tweets all day long. If I want to know something, checking her feed will tell me.

Emery's phone rings before I can answer, and she holds up her index finger, indicating she wants me to wait. "Hello ...? Hello?" She hangs up. "Unknown caller. I've been getting a ton of sales calls lately. It's starting to piss me off. Okay, you were saying?"

"Yep. That's why the job, babe. Gotta get my funds back in order. Savings is good, but it won't last forever."

"Thank Christ. If I have to hear my parents going at it one more time, I'm going to lose my shit. Ever since my mother got the clean bill of health and the cancer is officially gone, they're like rabbits on crack. I kid you not." She complains, but deep down, I know she loves that her parents have that kind of relationship. She's told me many times. I can't blame her.

From my perspective, living with my folks the past few months, I feel her pain. It's one of the many reasons I need out of mine. Being there gives me too much time to think. Think about my life and what needs to be done to get it back on track.

"Set up a showing, and we can sign. All my stuff is in storage. We have everything we need there. I have an extra bed, too, if you need it."

When she shakes her head, I glare at her through the mirror. One thing you don't do when a woman has lifter and a brush is move your head.

"Sorry." She stills. "I'm good. I have that under control. You think they're going to let us?"

I hold the foil and spread on the lightener with a brush, then fold the foil up into a packet, pushing it on her head. "We're adults."

Emery bursts out laughing, with me following right behind. "Right. The place has a very secure system, the guy on the phone said. We can have Buzz and Breaker check it out to make sure."

"That'd be good."

She calls my name, and I look at her in the mirror.

"Is it safe for you?"

Emotions well at the surface, threatening to come out, but I gather my strength and bury them deep, where they need to stay. "Of course. At least, it is with my Glock." On a wink, I return to her hair then set her under the dryer to process.

She's right. My father is Cruz, President of the Ravage MC Motorcycle Club here in Sumner, Georgia. Many fear him, but never me. At least, not yet. He's strict in what he expects, but I've learned he's fair. He and I are very close. If you looked up daddy's little girl in the dictionary, my picture would be there. It doesn't mean he's going to like me moving out on my own again.

I wash Emery's hair, cut, and then blow dry it.

"We need a plan."

You know that old saying, asking forgiveness is easier than asking for permission? Once it's done, they can't argue but so much. That's what part of my plan is, anyway.

Her brow quirks in that way she does when we're up to something and she's all in, no matter what it is. That's what I love about her. She's always along for the ride.

She's the kind of friend I could call and she would be ready to hide the body without a single question as to why or whom. That's more than a friend or a cousin; it's a sister.

"Hear me out. My father will probably have issues with me having my own place. Even in The Brookshire. I say we keep it to ourselves and sign the lease. Then we can tell both our families before we move, and hopefully they won't blow a gasket."

The Brookshire is one of the nicer apartment complexes in Sumner. It has extra security upon entering and exiting the property. It's not what Ravage could set up, but it's better than nothing.

"We're twenty-one and twenty-years-old," she tells me, something I already know, and says nothing more.

"Yeah, I know how old I am, Emery. Doesn't mean they'll roll with it." My father is super protective. I get that, but I need my own space. It's imperative.

"Let's do it," she says, rising from the chair.

I snap off the cape as she runs her fingers through her hair, letting it fall down her back.

"I love it. Thank God you're back!"

Yep. I'm back, in more ways than one.

CHAPTER TWO

Austyn

"Come eat!" my mother, Princess Cruz, calls from the mouth of the hallway that leads down to my childhood bedroom.

I close the box and tape the top of it. I've been going at this all day with my door closed. Now, it's time to tell them.

I'm nervous, not going to lie, but I'm going to tackle them both at once. I figure that will make things go easier, at least in the long run. The lease is signed, deposit and first month's rent is down. The place is ours, and I'm ready to get on with my life and my plan.

I make my way to the kitchen, taking in the house on the way. My mom doesn't do flashy. Everything in her home is very down to earth and casual. The kitchen is large, the cabinets a rustic wooden color. The walls are painted cream, but then she has vibrant prints on one of the walls with pictures of her three kids on the other. The table fits eight people, but it can be expanded out if needed. It's home, and I've always loved it here. It will be a great place to visit. Yes, visit, not stay.

"There you are. What have you been doing cooped up in that room all day?" my mother asks, standing by the stove as she puts spaghetti on plates.

Princess is beautiful and doesn't look like she's in her later forties at all. If anything, she looks like she's my age. With her vibrant red streaks in her dark black hair, she stands out in a crowd. My mother would stand out, anyway, but the hair makes it no contest.

I bet Lexa did her hair in the last few weeks. I'm not sure how I feel about that, but now that I'm back, I'll do it.

"Need help?" I ask instead of answering, not quite ready to explain. Plus, I want my father here. Two birds, one stone and all.

"Sure." She hands me a plate, and I put meat sauce on top of the noodles, then a piece of garlic toast on the side.

"Smells good," my father's deep voice comes from the entrance of the kitchen. He walks to the table, sitting down in his spot.

I carry the plate over and put it in front of my father.

He looks up at me, love in his eyes. "Thank you, baby girl."

With a smile on my face and warmth in my heart, I make my way back over to my mother who hands me another plate that I do the same thing to then sit next to my father.

The food looks good and smells good, but inside, butterflies have decided to take a hit of crack and have a party in my belly, unsure of how my parents will take the news. I've been here for months under their watchful eye. Now this will change. A change they had to know would arrive at some point.

When my mother joins us, we dig in. We're not a family that is particular about manners. Belching is a norm, mostly by my two brothers when they're here and my father. My mom always says it's a compliment to her cooking, considering she couldn't cook for shit back in the day and had to learn. It was a running joke when we were little because, if it weren't for takeout, we'd have starved.

"This weekend, I want you at the clubhouse," my father springs on me, making me stop the fork midway to my mouth.

I haven't been to the clubhouse in three and a half months. It's not because I was angry or upset with anyone; I just haven't wanted to deal with it. Deal with the questions or the looks of pity since everyone knows what happened to me. Fuck that.

My parents have been pretty lenient about my attendance at family functions, which I'm grateful for. Judging from my mother's demeanor and the sternness in her face, this isn't going to be one of those times where I'm going to get out of it. Between her and my father, they're going to strong arm me.

The timing is a bit sooner than I thought-out, but I'll make it work. It's time.

"Sure thing."

My mother's fork clatters to her plate, the sudden noise giving me a little jolt. "Seriously?"

"Yeah, Mom. It's fine. I'm back to work and getting my life in order. It's time to move on."

A smile graces her face. "This is good. I'm proud of you, Austyn." My mother has always been on my side, my biggest cheerleader in life. I'm hoping that'll prove true with what I'm about to lay on them. With me agreeing to go back into the fold so readily, it may lessen the blow.

"Emery and I got a place at The Brookshire, and we're going to move in tomorrow."

My mother stares at me, dumbfounded.

My father glares, which was expected.

Silence falls over the room as the air gets sucked out of it. The tension becomes so thick it's almost making me rethink my decision. Almost.

I can only be thankful Nox, Cooper, and his woman, Bristyl, aren't here to add their two cents to the mix. That would only add to my discomfort. No more of that is needed.

"It's time for me to get on with my life and not live in the past." Gripping the napkin, it tears and breaks into smaller pieces, but there is no stopping.

My father pushes away from the table and crosses his arms, looking very imposing. "That fucker is still out there. He had you tied to a table and stuck blades in you. Repeatedly. And you want me to let you out of my sight?" The pain in his eyes is stark, his features tight.

He doesn't need to remind me of what happened. I remember every agonizing second of it.

Memories flood my mind. The pain. The fear. The unknown. The way *he* looked at me, smiling as *he* pushed the knife inside my flesh slowly so it would be more painful. I still feel those moments when the metal entered my flesh.

The man hates me, but not as much as I hate him.

"I lived it, Dad."

His eyes soften just a touch at my tone and words. He was at my side while I recovered and saw the pain that man inflicted. He heard me cry and had to cover my wounds after adding ointment to them. My father is a man who likes control, and him not getting that, not having *him*, has been eating at him. I know it.

"I know, and I'm sure as hell never going to let you go through that again. We're working on finding him, but he's gone ghost."

The club has been searching for *him* since it happened. That's what my brothers Nox and Cooper, who are patched members of the club, have told me. They couldn't tell me anymore because it's club business, even though it's also my business.

Since no one said anything about finding *him,* I suspected this would make things harder.

"I get that, but I can't let *him* win. Being cooped up in this house isn't living. Me working. Having my own place. Going to the clubhouse for family things. That's me living."

"We get that, Austyn," my mother finally speaks. "But *he* could come at any moment, and we won't know."

I think fast, knowing this opportunity could be slipping through my fingers. It isn't an option I can lose. My parents are great, but they are demanding, as well.

"The apartment has a security system, and we were thinking Buzz and Breaker could come and amp it up. If you wanted, they could put cameras on the outside of the place to watch who comes and goes." This is a bit of a stretch, but if it will make this happen, I'll suck it up. As long as the cameras aren't inside the apartment, watching my every move, I'll be good.

"Why is this so important to you?" my mother asks softly, which is not her style one bit. She's more straight to the point and in your face. Her being on the gentle side tugs at my heart.

"I'm taking my life back, Mom. What *he* did to me, I can't change. What I can control is what I do now." In more ways than one. This is just the first major step.

21

"I should put you on lockdown," my father grunts out, and my stomach falls like a lead weight.

Being on lockdown at the clubhouse will ruin everything. Not being able to leave the compound and having all the brothers watching me all the time is not an option at this point. Having the cameras at the new place is a stretch, but this can't happen.

"No, no lockdown, Dad."

He studies me for long moments, face blank, not giving me anything. I feel it slipping away—my control—and I hate it. I need it back to feel whole again.

"I—"

"I'm having the guys go full-out with security," he cuts me off. "They will monitor the place twenty-four seven." He runs his hand through his dark hair that has a little more salt in it than it did a few weeks ago, giving it a tug. "Fuck, I can't believe I'm letting you do this shit. If I have one inkling that *he's* in town, you're on lockdown, no questions asked. Something isn't right, your ass is at the clubhouse."

That isn't good, but I'll take it ... for now.

Relief falls over me like a warm rain. "I'll take it."

Step two of the plan—check.

CHAPTER THREE

RYKER

"Last one," I call out to the guys as we pack for the next shipment the club is handling. It'll only be a day trip for this one, and Tug and Jacks are fulfilling it.

Screwing the screws on top of the crate, it's finished and ready to roll.

"On it." Cooper comes up with Nox not too far behind. They lift the crate and take it to the box truck out front.

It was by sheer luck I found the Ravage MC. Living on the streets was hard, but I found myself a job and a place to live. The problem was, I still wasn't happy, and being pissed off at the world doesn't help a man.

GT and Dagger were in a bar I attended regularly. They started bullshitting with me in a way that was comfortable, like I'd known them for years. We got to talking about the club, but they were pretty vague. They reiterated how it was focused around family. It was a time in my life when I needed that one thing—family.

And that's what the Ravage MC is, and it's what they have given me. Men and women who stand by each other through thick and thin, who have each other's backs, who give a shit, who truly care. It's more than I've had in years.

I hopped on my ride and never looked back, following GT and Dagger to a family worth a damn.

I reach in and grab a smoke, pulling one out and tapping the end of it. The tip rests on my lips as I light it, inhaling the tobacco and nicotine as Rhys comes by and takes a seat next to me at an old picnic table.

"How ya doin'?" he asks, folding his hands in front of him, not looking at me.

Rhys is one badass motherfucker. Seeing him in action makes everyone else look like pussies. He's a great man to have at your back, which is the only place you want him.

Exhaling the smoke, I tell him, "Same shit, different day, brother."

"You got anything?"

Immediately, I know what he's asking, and I fucking hate that he has to ask.

Anger stirs in my blood, pulsing and awakening. He's the man who kidnapped Austyn from her own damn home and hurt her. Dickhead will pay for that.

"Airport outside of Dunham, JK has a plane, but it hasn't moved since he went under. Tapped all the phone lines of his family, and the only one I can tell he talks to is his mother, but not often. He's withdrawing money, but somehow the only paper trail for it is the amount of the withdraws. There is no location or precise bank

24

information."

Rhys rubs his thumb over his lip. "Smart fucker."

Inhaling another drag, I say, "Yeah. Buzz and I went and wired up the house, but he hasn't shown up there, either. Wherever he is, he's in deep."

"Time to get the rat to come out of the hole."

I've been busting my ass to find information on the man who took and hurt Austyn. He fell through my fingers. When we found her, I was more concerned with her as blood ran down her body to the floor. It's a vision I wish would leave my memory banks, yet it has embedded itself there like a static movie that won't end.

She's made it her mission to turn me away every time I go to visit her. Instead of wasting my time on her parents' porch, which is what I did for weeks, I put it to good use by trying to find this man. That was after a little conversation with Deke that ended up with us both pissed and me needing to find some direction to channel all of it.

"And how do you suppose we do that?"

A sinister smile plays on his lips. "Don't know yet, but I'll figure it out."

I take another drag and blow out the smoke. "We all need to figure this shit out. It's been months."

My first thought was he left the country, which is still a possibility. What changes my mind on that scenario is the money withdrawals. If they were done in a foreign country, there would be more of a paper trail. Slight, but still there. This makes me think he's still in the US.

The door swings open and Cruz walks in, striding to us. "We all set?"

I stub out my smoke. "Yep. Coop and Nox are loading, and it's ready."

"Good."

"I'm out," Rhys says, standing up and tapping once on the table. Goodbyes are called out as he disappears. That's Rhys. He comes in, gets the information, and then he's smoke.

Cruz parks his ass on the bench in front of me, bringing his finger and thumb to the corners of his mouth and then down. "Tell me again why I didn't beat your ass for sitting on my porch, waiting for my little girl?"

A chuckle escapes. Leave it to Cruz to make it into a joke. "Because you loved seein' my sexy face every day."

He scoffs. "My ass."

"Is there a point to this conversation?" Because normally, he doesn't bring up his daughter with me. At least, he hasn't for a while now.

Cruz lifts his brows. "Yeah. Just lettin' you know I notice. I see. I hear. My eyes are wide fuckin' open when it comes to my baby girl."

I reach in for another smoke, tap it out, and light it up. "And this has changed since I joined?"

Cruz loves his kids. He'd lay down his life for any of them, no questions asked. He's also protective as fuck, especially of his little girl.

"Nope, just thought I'd remind ya." He taps on the wood then rises from the table. "Gotta head out. We're movin' Austyn and Emery into their new place."

This catches my attention, and I rise with him, meeting him eye for eye. "What?"

Austyn is safe in her parents' home, not out on her own when I don't know where this fucker is.

26

"Wants to get her life back in order."

"And you let her move out?" I'm stunned and shocked beyond measure. At least while she was there, he and Princess could keep tabs on her. Now ... fuck.

"She's serious about it, and I want her straight again. She's been locked up inside herself for months and is now coming out." He sighs heavily. "Buzz went and wired the place last night. We have cameras on the outside that are monitored all the time."

"Fuck, I don't like this."

He crosses his arms over his chest and a menacing, determined look comes across his face. "Yeah, and why do you have a right to not like somethin' when it involves my daughter?"

The man is fishing. I'm surprised it's taken him this long. He's a man who needs to be in the know and makes no qualms about it. Thing is, I'm a man, too, and it's time.

Looking him square in the eye, I say, "Been mine for a long damn time, brother."

"Hurt her and I kill you." He taps the table two times then walks out of the building.

I collapse back down, letting out a deep breath.

I've never made a play for a woman. Never had to. However, with Austyn blocking me out these past few months, I'm going to have to make a play. Probably several of them.

Green, one of my brothers, walks in, holding a notebook and pen.

"Green!" I call over to him, and he makes his way to me.

"What's up?" He sets the paper down.

"Not that I want to ask you this shit, but I need to."

His eyes hide a ghost that I was afraid would appear when this topic was brought up. He's not a dumb man. Far from it.

"Leah, she went through what Austyn did with those fuckers? Or similar?"

Leah is best friends with Bristyl, Cooper's woman, which is how she and Green hooked up. Bristyl had some guys after her back in Florida who used Leah to get to her. Leah was tied to a bed, and the guys took turns on her, not sexually, but physically, carving into her body. When she was found, she was a bloody mess and in hysterics. The only person who could even get through to her on any level was Green.

After that, she moved up here to Sumner, not wanting to be anywhere near Florida. She has her own place, but Green stays with her pretty much every night.

Green clenches his hands. "Yeah."

I meet his eyes. "Brother, I wouldn't ask this if it wasn't important."

He nods once, saying nothing else.

"Can Austyn get through this? I mean, I don't know shit about what to do."

Green shakes his head then rubs his finger and thumb over his lips. "She can. It takes a shitload of time and someone being there for her. It's shit, all of it, but yeah. Leah is slowly comin' back to herself. I don't know if she'll ever be the same, but she's claiming her life back piece by piece. Austyn'll do the same, I imagine."

"What can I do?"

A slight smirk tips his lips. "Be there for her. Be her friend."

"Friend?"

"Yeah. Shitty, but that's what Leah needed, and not some hound dog trying to get in her pants. Be friends, and the rest of it will flow. Be patient and understanding. And demanding things from her will only piss her off more. See, Leah didn't have any control, so she started to grasp at things she could. It was a coping mechanism. I let her do what she had to do."

We stare at each other for a moment as he picks up his paper. "Look, brother, it's not easy, but it'll happen in time. Gotta go."

"Right. Thanks." I hang my head briefly. Austyn has been through so much, but damn if she isn't always on my mind.

I look at my watch, jump up, and head to my bike. I call out goodbyes as I turn over my ride and take off. An hour later, I'm pulling up to my mother's house, or what could be called a house. More like a rundown piece of shit shack her "husband" put her in.

The siding is from the nineteen-seventies and probably has asbestos or some shit in it. It's gray and pieces are hanging off everywhere. The porch is a slab of concrete with parts of it cracked off. Regardless, she tries making do with what she has by planting flowers and shrubs around the place, taking some of the damage away.

Killing the bike, I make my way to the front door that opens immediately.

My mother looks worn down and tired. Her eyes have no spark, and the lines around her face are showing signs of aging.

"Matthew," she greets, holding the rickety door open for me, and I step through.

The inside of the place isn't any better than the outside. Holes are in the flooring and walls, exposing wood underneath them. I know if I go into the bathroom, it will be full of mold and mildew. She lives in shit. And she wants to live in shit, which is her choice.

I look around, searching for her husband. It's more for show than actuality because I wouldn't be here if he was.

"Whatnot hanging out with wives three, twelve, and twenty-four today?"

"Matthew, that's enough." Her scold is nothing to me, though I bet it works on my siblings. They're stuck, and that is something that scrapes my balls.

A chuckle escapes. "Just stating the obvious."

"You have no right to dictate my life." She looks me up and down, the corner of her lip rising. "I mean, look at you."

Holding my arms out wide, I let her have a good look. "What ya see is what ya get, Ma."

"Do you have it?" Her question comes out fast as she peers out the window, no doubt looking for anyone who might see my bike in the driveway. She lives in a well-populated neighborhood, but I'd bet my right nut no one knows what goes on behind these closed doors.

"What? No hug?"

Her eyes narrow briefly, but she catches herself, sucking in a deep breath. "I'm sorry. It's just been a long time."

"Two months, Ma, and you still won't let me see my brothers and sisters." There are six of them, and it's been years since I've been allowed to see them or talk to them. Seventeen to be exact.

"James doesn't feel it's a good idea." She moves around her small house, beginning to pick up some magazines and organize them on the small table in front of the couch.

"And we always do what he says, right?" That's just a small part of it. My sperm donor is a piece of shit in every sense of the word. I can't fucking stand him, yet my mother seems to love him. Truth is, I think she's brainwashed to do so.

She's been with him for over thirty years. That does a lot to a woman's mentality. Considering she's only forty-nine, that's some sick shit right there. She had me at eighteen, her first.

"He's my husband. It's ordained. It's faith. God chose, and this is the path we are meant to take," she protests, pulling up to her small height, her chin up.

Not a lot I admire about my mother anymore, but her determination is still there. He hasn't completely destroyed that yet, but it will happen in time. If only she'd just change her mind and get out.

"Yeah, you and what is it, four, eight, twelve? It's been a long time since we've had this conversation; his numbers have to be up there."

"How many sister-wives I have isn't your business, Matthew. I appreciate your help—we all do—but you can't come in here and dictate our lives."

Crossing my arms, I stare at the woman who brought me into this world, took care of me, worked three jobs, and still does to put food on the table, and who read me stories before bed when she could.

Her tired eyes droop, and I can't help wondering when was the last time she had a good night's sleep. She's probably up worrying about her asshat and what he's doing with his other "wives." He's not really married to them. Instead, he says they are "spiritual soul mates," whatever the fuck that means. He only has one wife who he's legally bound to, and it isn't my mother, who's number two.

"You know, I don't give a shit how many women want to put up with that fucker. Hell, the more the merrier. What I care about is the fucked-up mess you're putting my brothers and sisters in. When your biological father is also your uncle, that shit is fucked up and twisted." That's just one of the fucked-up things going on in this cult. Yeah, that's what it is. I don't give a shit who says any different. Living it, I have a right to my opinions.

My biological father's, mom's husband, first wife is my aunt, my mother's sister who is two years older than her. Yeah, so my fucking cousins are also my half-siblings. That shit is wacked. I'm down with a lot of stuff in this life, but that isn't one of them.

Tears pool in her eyes, but she doesn't allow them to fall. Another thing is, she's strong.

"Breanna turns sixteen in a couple of months," she reminds me.

Anger burrows as the bottom of my stomach falls to the ground like a brick. Fear has hit me a few times in my life. Seeing Austyn tied up was definitely one of them. Breanna turning sixteen is another.

Taking a step closer, her eyes lift to mine.

"Don't let it happen, Ma. I'm serious as a heart attack. You're the only one who can stop it and make this right."

My heart feels as if a machete is having a fun time piercing through it as the past comes back to rock me on my heels. Guilt lays at my feet and eats me from the inside out.

I'd lost touch with my mother for a while because I was pissed as hell at her. During that time, shit happened that I can never change. That's on me. I can't let the same thing happen to Breanna. Not remembering her birthday is on me too. The weight on my shoulders gets heavier.

"It's already in the works, Matthew, and you have no say."

The robotic way she says those words eats at me. That's him talking, not her. After this long, she just thinks it is. That pisses me off. She may as well be one of those zombies on that damn television show Cooper's woman likes to watch.

"No. She deserves to choose who she wants to be with in this life.

Not the other way around, and definitely not a fucking cousin, uncle, or what-the-fuck-ever-else he concocts. That shit is not right, and you know it. You saw Samantha go through it. You can't want that for Breanna. You can stop this."

She gives out a loud sigh. "No, I can't. It's time for you to go."

"You want me to take my money with me?"

Fear and panic crosses her features as her hand goes up to her neck. I know she needs it. She always needs it because her piece of shit husband doesn't provide for her and my siblings. It baffles me why she stays, why she puts up with his shit. But, at this point, there's nothing I can do. She continues to work her ass off for nothing; that's her choice.

"Please, Matthew." Her words are whispered, and I hate that, as well. If I could give her a fucking backbone, I would.

Reaching in my pocket, I pull out the wad of money and hold it out to her. She takes it quickly, as if it's a mirage and if she doesn't get it that moment, it will disappear. Truth, I'd give it to her, anyway. She needs it. My siblings need it.

I'm the oldest. Then there is Samantha, who is twenty-five and married off. Breanna, who's turning sixteen. Ashley, who's eleven. Brian, who's nine. And Adam, the youngest, is seven. It's a huge age gap, and with my mom's age now, she doesn't need to be popping out any more.

"Right. It's been fun." I turn and walk through the door, knowing my time here is done.

It always ends this way, because she chooses it to. Once, I thought she might just have the balls to actually let me see my brothers and sisters, but that was just hope, the one thing with my family a person should not have.

"Thank you," she says as I face her again.

"I'm fuckin' serious about Breanna. You *can* do something. You're not helpless." My look turns icy. By her small gasp, she sees it.

Saying nothing else, I get the fuck out of there.

It's the fucking truth. I'll do whatever it takes to get my sister out of that shit. Samantha was already gone before I could, but Breanna ... she won't live this shit if she doesn't want to.

My phone pings with a text.

Carley: *I want to party.*

Me: *And ...*

Carley: *Pick me up.*

Me: *And do what with you?*

Carley: *Take me to the clubhouse, idiot.*

I chuckle, sending her a text about the party coming up and that I'll pick her up for it. My cousin got out of this cult life a couple of years ago and looked me up. It took her a while to get her head on straight after being with all those fuckers for so long, but she's adjusted well and loves to party.

Personally, I don't give a fuck. She wants to screw my club brothers, so be it. At least I know she's safe.

Funny how life decides to toss shit in your face, but keeps right on moving. At least Carley was able to shake it off her and live a life that she wants. It's my job to make sure Breanna gets that chance too.

I'll do whatever it takes for family.

CHAPTER FOUR

Austyn

"That goes in my bedroom," Emery directs her brother and my older cousin, Deke, in our new apartment. Buzz and Breaker, who are techy kings, came in and did their thing, then taught us how to work the system. We have remotes on our phones and everything. Neither Emery nor I can see the cameras, but we know they're here.

The entire time we've been moving, all I've gotten out of Deke is a grunt. One was when he got here, acknowledging my existence. At least there's that, even if it's not much.

Pulling him aside and talking to him is a must, but not with all these people around. Love my family, but some things are better left unknown. Some things, you take to the grave.

I haven't talked to Deke since *it* happened, and I feel guilty for that. He blames himself for the fucker coming at me, but that's just not the case. He doesn't need to hold that burden; the asshole who hurt me does. He's one of the few I truly trust, and his avoidance hurts, but I have no one to blame but myself.

"How much shit do you need?" my oldest brother Cooper asks, carrying one end of the couch.

"Yeah, there's, like, two other couches down there. Where're they gonna go?" my twin brother Nox says from the other end of the couch. Got to love brothers. Or, at least their strong arms.

"Let me educate you. This is a couch, the smaller one downstairs is a loveseat, and the other is a recliner. They aren't all couches." I point to where the piece needs to go, and they set it down not so gently.

"Let me educate you." Nox leans in threateningly, not that he scares me, though it would to normal people.

I just stop myself from the eye roll.

Being twins, we have a special connection, yet he gives me shit whenever possible. It must be in the brother rulebook or something.

"I don't give a flyin' fuck what's what. Once this shit gets up here, I'm out."

I tap the side of his face. "Aw, love you, too, baby brother."

"By one fuckin' minute! And you still bust my damn balls about it," he gripes, but he's not pissed. It's something we joke about regularly. I was born before, yes briefly, but it counts, and holding it over him is for pure entertainment purposes.

"Nice goat." I move my hand back and forth in the air next to me like I'm petting a goat at my feet.

Cooper chuckles. This is an inside joke between the three of us and our parents. It's a play off the *got your goat* saying that I heard growing up from my grandpa, Pops. Whenever any of us snags the other in a verbal blow, we make a deal about it and say *nice goat.*

"Fuck off," Nox says with a smile then heads back out the door.

Looking around at our new place, I take in the light cream walls in the wide-open space that is the kitchen, living, and dining areas. The recessed lighting along the ceiling adds to the warm feel. There is no fireplace, which in Georgia, who needs one? Though, there is a very large balcony off the living room area where we can fit a couple of chairs for relaxation.

When we first walked in, it was pretty bland, but now, with our things coming in and getting placed around the room, it's coming alive.

Mine and Emery's parents show up and help out, but I specifically asked that no one else from the club come. It's not that I don't want to see them. It's just the questions they are dying to ask. Moving on is hard enough with all the bullshit that could come along with it.

After pizza and beer, I make my move to Deke, sucking in a deep breath as I do. Cooper already left and some of the others are starting to get up, too, but Deke needs to stay.

Sliding up to him, I ask, "Can you stay for a few after?"

"After what?"

Deke is a rock of a man. He used to be an underground fighter and was estranged from the family for years, until I went to him for help. Dragging him home didn't make him happy, and me shutting him out these past few of months really hasn't made him any happier, or so Emery's told me.

When we got home, Deke had to face a lot of shit from his father. Then he learned that his mother had cancer. Not to mention the club and coming to terms with the reason he left in the first place, namely JK. It wasn't an easy road for him, and I added to that hardship.

As much as I wanted to talk to him before, something held me back. It's time to clear that up.

I look up at him. "They leave. Can we go somewhere to talk?"

He pulls out his phone, looking at the time. "Need to be back to Rylie in an hour. Let's go now."

"Right."

When we leave, nothing is said by anyone except for goodbyes. I hop into his monster of a truck, and he fires it up. It feels like old times.

"Where are we going?" I ask in a rush when I wake up to find we are flying down the road in Deke's truck.

"Home."

*Anger bubbles inside me, along with a twinge of fear. "You asshole! You told me I could stay with you." I move to get the seatbelt off, only thinking one thing—*must get out of this truck.

He reaches over and grabs my arm, tightly holding me in place. Damn man is too strong for his own good. "No, I said you could stay last night. Already called Nox, and he's expecting us."

"Fuck, Deke, do you have any idea what you've done?" I groan, falling back to the seat and dropping my head onto the back window with a thump. The cramps in my stomach are no match for the pounding of my heart. "I'm fucking dead."

"Shoulda thought of that before you hopped in a car with someone you didn't fuckin' know. That's some stupid shit right there, Austyn. Know you're smarter than that."

I sigh heavily. There's so much he doesn't know and he would have had he returned home at any point in the last four years. "Fuck, Deke, you have no idea what you've done. You have no idea what's going on."

"Fuckin' enlighten me so I know what I'm gettin' myself into."

He's right. He's driving me back home to a place he doesn't want to be. I owe him something. Not all, but something, even if I don't want to give it. My insides ache.

My voice softens. "I lied."

He slams on the brakes, and I put my arms out to the dash to brace myself, my head moving forward with the truck. I blow the hair out of my face in a huff.

"What?" he clips, anger pulsating out of him.

Knowing I'm too late, I still say, "Don't get pissed."

"Too fuckin' late. Talk."

Pain hits me hard in the gut as an emptiness inside me makes its presence known. I'm hollow, vacant, a void. My heart is strangling just at the thought of telling him.

"You can't tell anyone, Deke. I'm confiding in you. I can't let anyone know why I was in Grayson." I picked that town for the sole purpose of going to Deke afterward, but nothing ever seems to go as planned.

"Talk!" he barks, making me jump in shock.

"Deke," I snip back. "I mean it. This is serious shit."

"Talk. I'll decide." From the look on his face as he stares at me, he's not going to let this go. I opened that door, and now I have to walk through it.

"You're not gonna let me go unless I tell you ..." My thoughts trail off, and I pause for a few moments, getting all my thoughts in line. "I didn't hitchhike. I'm not stupid. I took the Greyhound here, not wanting the tracker in my car to keep tabs on me."

"Well, at least you have some sense."

I let out a huff. "If you'd have been around the last four years, you never would've bought the hitchhike thing in the first place. I needed to do something, and it couldn't be in Sumner. Emery told me a while back where you were living, so I planned that something here so I could crash with you for a couple days."

A vein throbs in his throat, and his breathing is deep, telling me he's pissed. "What something? And don't fucking blow rainbows up my ass, woman."

I'm unable to hide the small smirk that comes to my lips. No matter the situation, I've learned to take the small joys, and Deke just gave me one.

"We've missed you."

"Austyn ..." he warns.

No one knows this. Not a single soul on the planet, yet here I am, just going to tell Deke after he hasn't been around for four years. When in the depths of Hell, one can hope for a lifeline. Deke might just be mine. Something tells me, though, that I can trust him. That I have to trust him.

I clear my throat, fighting back all the emotions and confusion inside me. "Let's just say, yesterday, when I came to town, I was pregnant. Today, I'm not."

"What?" His voice dips and shock comes to his eyes.

My head whips toward him, tears and anger burning in my eyes. The pain of not having my child inside me squeezes my heart to the point of pain. Instead of letting it show, though, I let the anger win. Anger is a much better emotion. It doesn't show weakness, at least not all the time. "I'm not talking about it anymore, Deke. You got more than I wanted to give."

"What about your face?"

My fists clench at remembering that fucker and his smug look when I came out. "You should see him. Fucker outside the clinic said I was a murderer. Said I didn't deserve to breathe. Said I was a whore. He came at me, and I didn't think he was actually going to hit me, but he did. I fought back, of course, but he got a couple licks in." My body vibrates, but I will my hands to relax. It works, somehow.

"So, let me get this straight; you just had a procedure, and you're out beating the ass of some asshole?"

"Yeah, Deke. That's why I passed out at your place. They gave me some painkillers, and I took them after I got out of the cab at your place." I needed them, and they knocked me out, but that was the whole point of taking them and finding Deke. He was my safe place to crash and work through the aftermath.

"Fuck, Austyn. Why didn't you tell me this yesterday instead of fuckin' lyin'?"

"No one knows I was pregnant. I mean, no one except now you. You think I want anyone in our family to find out what I did? They'll be pissed. But I couldn't keep it." My breaths come out short, and tears prick the back of my eyes. It takes everything in me not to let them fall. Not because I'm ashamed, but because I miss my baby.

"Who's the father?"

"That, I'm not discussing."

My stomach twists as I allow my mind to go back there.

He stood by my side through coming home and dealing with the family, who still don't know I was pregnant. All because Deke kept my secret.

Deke drives as I turn toward him, needing to get this over with so we can move on. I don't want this between us anymore.

"I'm sorry," I start, and he looks over at me briefly then back to the windshield. He has one hand on the top of the steering wheel, doing that cool man move. It works on him. Hell, everything works on him. He's the badass cousin. "I shouldn't have shut you out, but at the time, it was the only way I could deal. I already didn't have my baby and was dealing with that. After what happened, I had to block everything else out. It wasn't you, Deke. It was everyone ... Everything."

"Not Emery. You didn't block her," the man of few, yet always important, words says.

I shake my head. "No, not Emery." I needed her, even it if was to cry on her shoulder. She spent many nights with me curled up in bed. Most of the time, I didn't sleep, only stared at the walls, hollow. Scrubbing myself in the shower never made the dirt go away because it was on the inside. It's still there, festering. The dirt *he* laid upon me feeds my beast inside, ready to exact retribution.

"She know about the baby?"

I jump out of my thoughts, feeling this strange twinge in my chest. I haven't talked about the baby with anyone but Deke, and that was a while ago. Talking about it now feels foreign and scary.

"No. No one knows, Deke. Unless you told someone ..." I trail off. He's giving me the look of death, like how dare I even think he'd break my confidence. Knowing him now, it's true. I really didn't believe for a second he would. He's not that kind of man.

He pulls the truck off to the side of the road and throws it in park. "You know how much shit I got from the brothers for not sayin' anything. How I kept that from them because you asked me not to tell. Rylie doesn't know. Not a fuckin' soul, Austyn."

I exhale a breath I didn't know I was holding. Him keeping something from his brothers and his woman is a huge deal. It speaks of courage, honor, and loyalty. Deke has that in spades, making me like him even more.

"Thank you."

"Yeah, thanks." I don't miss the sarcastic tone in his voice. "What that fucker did to you is on me. Your dad tell you what happened and the reasons?"

I nod, feeling the punch. "A little. Just that you were young, and *he* was your dealer. *He* threatened us kids if you didn't go away and stay away."

"Exactly. I came back, and this is what happens." He shakes his head.

It feels like there is a lead weight in my stomach, threatening to take me down to the ground. I want to throw up. I want to scream. He's wrong. So very wrong. But if I tell him what happened before, he'll carry more on his shoulders. He doesn't need that. I can carry that for him. He's already held too much for too long.

"No, Deke, you can't blame yourself for this shit. He's a sick sonofabitch."

His eyes turn scary. So much so I take a breath and arch my back toward the window.

"I'll find him, and when I do, I'll fuckin' destroy him."

I understand exactly where he's coming from, just in a different way. While I want Deke to get his revenge, there's something I need too. I have to close this once and for all.

"You have to promise me that you won't blame yourself for what happened. It's over and done with. No more of that shit." Guilt slams its ugly head at not telling him everything, but I've already made my decision on that.

He shakes his head. "Not how this works, Austyn. You know it. I know it. Eye for an eye. Until I have him on a bed, spread eagle with my knife going into his flesh, it's not over."

I full-out cringe at the thought, and the slight scars on my body begin to tingle just knowing he's talking about them. "I'm sorry, Deke."

"Not one damn thing for you to be sorry for, Austyn. Just don't hide from me anymore. Family sticks together, no matter what."

"Right." It kills me that I'm hiding something.

This may have to be a race. One against time. One I intend to win. I have to find JK first.

CHAPTER FIVE

Austyn

The clubhouse is exactly the same as before my life was flipped upside down for the second time. Not one thing has changed. It's home. Even as I think that, a small part of me is apprehensive about how people will treat me or what they will say.

Pulling up, I wave out the car window, and then the gates glide open. The lot is filled with cars and trucks on the right and bikes on the left. The shop, Banner Automotive, sits off to the back right while the clubhouse sits off to the left.

I park the car, and Emery bounces up. She had family things to do and needed to come early, which is why I'm driving myself. Me, I really didn't want to come early.

Emery wraps her arms around me and pulls me into a hug as soon as my feet hit the pavement. "I'm so happy you're here."

"Girl, I told you I was coming."

"I know." She pulls away and looks deeply into my eyes, showing her meaning. She's happy I'm back. That after I'd been lost for a while and between my job, apartment and this, I was back. "Come on."

I follow her into the clubhouse, getting hugs on the way, but not stopping for too much chitchat. The hard shell I placed over myself is in full-swing, but answering questions isn't something I want to do. To be asked anything isn't something my time needs to be spent on.

"You came," my mother states, coming out from around the bar, wearing tight, ripped jeans and a black Harley tank. Her hair is down, flowing around her, as beautiful as ever.

"You act like I'm going to bail on you or something."

She places her hand on her hip, in the don't-mess-with-me mom move. "Yeah. Like the other times I asked you to come and you bailed. Let's go find your father."

My dad stands just inside the main room of the clubhouse, his arms stretched open wide. I walk right into them, and he wraps them around me.

My father is a big man, tall and bulky, but in a muscular way. Even with the years he's packed on and dealing with three children, he looks good. I'm not saying that in a sick way, but in an I'm female and have eyes way.

"How's my baby girl doin'?" He kisses the top of my head.

"Good. Mom's giving me shit. Nothing new there."

He pulls away, smiling down at me. "I bet she is. And looks like she won, considering you're here."

I shrug. "Figured I'd let this one ride."

He chuckles deeply. "Yeah."

"Yeah, years of practice and all."

In reality, getting one over on my mother is harder than breaking out of a prison. This is me and my dad, though—joking, laughing, being us. It feels good to have that back after being closed up these past few months. Yes, it's definitely time to claim my life back.

"Years and years. Good to have ya here."

"Thanks, Dad."

He kisses the top of my head again before releasing me then going to my mother and kissing her roughly and deeply.

Their love is a once in a lifetime kind of thing. Growing up, watching it develop and come to life has made me want, at least at one time. The way my father sneaks touches, kisses, or even when he full-out doesn't care who's watching and takes my mother. The way they joke, their laughter filling our house with that enjoyment. They didn't have to fake it. Ever. Their connection was just there, strong and all-consuming.

When I was younger I'd do the *ew, gross* thing all the time, but as I grew older, I loved seeing that interaction between them. It made me hope and dream.

I had fantasies that I'd find a man just like my father one day. That he'd love me unconditionally, kissing me when he wanted, not caring who was around to see it, showing me his passion for me, and we'd form a bond that no one could break.

That's what they were, though. Fantasies. Because, a girl like me doesn't get those. A girl like me has to live in the moment. A girl like me has to deal with what life has thrown in my face. A girl like me doesn't get to have those touches. Not now. Coming to terms with that these last few months has been part of my challenge.

Life decided to throw me curveballs. It decided to kick me in the teeth while I was down. It decided to do it again, repeatedly, not letting up, holding me down. It's why I need to get back my control.

"Austyn!" Bristyl, my older brother Cooper's woman, calls from across the room, running toward me with her arms extended.

Guess today is going to be a day for hugging.

She wraps her arms around me. "You're here!!"

"That I am."

Bristyl and my brother have been together for a while. She's a pistol of a woman who has a strong business sense. She and my brother started managing storage units for the club. She used to manage some back where she's from, but now runs the club's. She was going to come help us move in, but something came up at work.

She pulls away, a wide smile gracing her face. "Come help Ma and me in the kitchen." She pulls me by the hand into the kitchen where my grandmother, who we call Ma, is whipping up food.

She turns to me and does the whole hug thing. "So happy to have your beautiful face here again." She gives me a squeeze, not asking questions.

This goes on for a while—the hugs and greetings. With as large as our family is, it takes hours. Luckily, I didn't get the *are you okay* question too many times.

It's not until hours later that I get my opportunity, deciding it's time. Taking back my life means I need to get information. And today is the day to get it. I have a reason to be at the clubhouse and an opportunity I can't let pass.

Moving quickly down the stairs to the basement, I make my way to the door I need. Turning the handle, I find it's locked, which is expected. I reach into my bag and pull out my lock picks, a present from

Tug, one of the brothers, who taught me how to use them.

Quickly and efficiently, I take care of the lock and open the door. Before me stands rows of computers and a hub. I shut the door, lock it, and move to the monitors.

Buzz taught me many things about computers and took lots of time with me in doing so because I showed interest. He just didn't know I'd be using his knowledge to hack into the Ravage system. I like to think of it more as gaining needed information from those I love. They're family and we're sharing information. It's a good way to look at it.

A hairdresser who can crack computers. No, I haven't put that on an application, but I may be able to find a good job for it. There should be something out there that would fit that bill.

I fire up the machines, knowing Buzz has it set up with a ton of security that I'll need to whittle through. It will take me some time, but I've been taught by the best.

I tried to do it from my apartment to avoid this, but the system won't allow me to get in remotely. Therefore, I needed to come to the central hub.

Buzz has the computers set to lock down if the wrong things are typed in, so I must be meticulous with my entries.

The floor above me creaks and groans with people dancing. A faint sound of music comes through, as well, and I find myself humming to the current song. I've always worked better with music. This is good because I don't have a lot of time, and I have to get it right.

Cracking computers has become second nature to me. It's like riding a bicycle. Even with months away, I can pick it right back up. Companies keep coming up with "special" ways to stop people from getting into each other's systems, but each of those is easier than the last. It's a joke.

It only takes me a few minutes before I'm in. I type in the search *JK Bridges*, my stomach coiling as the information is brought up. Files, spreadsheets, and documents line the finder. Not having time to go through it all right then, I insert the flash drive and download it all. It only takes minutes, then I put everything back exactly where I got it, leave the room, and lock it, joining everyone back upstairs.

When I first get to the top of the stairs, I look around, noting not one person even cared I was downstairs. Why would they? Sneaky, yes. But necessary for us all.

Sucking in a calming breath, I find Emery, Nox, Cooper, Bristyl, Deke, and Rylie sitting at a picnic table outside. I join them, feeling the flash in my pocket and wanting to get back to the apartment so I can look at it.

"Family givin' ya a hard time?" Nox asks with a grin. He and I have a good relationship. We don't have the connection that some twins have where we can read each other's feelings or any of that, but we're close.

"Nothing I didn't expect." Actually, I expected a lot worse; more of an interrogation of some sort. Luckily, that didn't happen.

"Hear you're back at work," Bristyl says, sitting next to Cooper. He has his arm around her waist, holding her securely to his body.

"Yep. You gonna come in and let me have at your hair?"

Her laugh is like velvet, soft yet a touch of rough. "Sure thing. I want pink or something fun."

"I can totally do that." I look at Nox, whose hair has grown very shaggy over the last few months.

He shakes his hair back with a grin. "Nah. I've gotta catch up to Coop here."

Cooper, the oldest of us all, has long hair he puts up in a man bun or ties at the nape of his neck. I've heard every woman who's ever encountered him swoon over the damn thing, gushing about how hot it is on him. He won't let me touch it, so it's become a running joke.

"You would rock the short, spiked hair look," I tease.

"You cut my hair, Austyn, and I'll kick your ass," he warns, and I know he's not joking. The man likes his hair, and Bristyl does, too, so it's a win-win. Truth, I wouldn't want to cut it, either. His hair is every woman's fantasy, except mine. No, it's nowhere close to mine.

A motorcycle roars in the distance, catching my attention, and I watch as Ryker speeds into the lot, a buxom blonde on the back, wrapped around him tightly. My stomach drops to the floor.

It's absolutely nothing new. I can't remember a time when Ryker didn't have a woman on his arm. He's ten years older than me, and my dumbass has had a thing for him for as long as I can remember. Watching him, craving him, lusting after him.

All of it was stupid. Is stupid.

Now that I've given up, it shouldn't sting so badly, yet it does.

My father told me that, while I was recovering, Ryker sat outside on the front porch, refusing to leave. I briefly thought maybe he had a thing for me, too, but seeing him now, with the woman wrapped around him like a glove … No. It doesn't matter, anyway. Ryker isn't going to happen. The sooner that gets through to my heart, the better off everyone will be.

The blonde climbs off, kisses Ryker's cheek, and then bounces off with a wide, satisfied smile. It's not the first I've seen and won't be the last.

It's like a train wreck. You know it's coming and you just have to watch anyway, cringing the entire time.

His focus zeroes in on me, and I know this because he tears his glasses away from his eyes and strides with purpose to where we're sitting.

His large frame blocks the sun as I look up, up, up at him. Damn, why does he have to be so attractive? There should be a law: no more hot guys allowed in the Ravage MC. Of course, he's already here so that does me zero bit of good.

Tattoos line his arms and neck intricately, like each one was placed in a specific spot for a specific reason. Each is detailed in ways that make them unique and stand out. I've had dreams of exploring each of them and finding out the stories behind them. Fantasies of him showing me exactly where the ones are that mean the most to him. Tracing them with my fingers and tongue. Moving over him while I take the canvas that is his body in. Again, those are all fantasies I had at one time.

Not anymore.

I no longer get that. Even if he wanted to and as much as it sucks, it's life.

"Austyn, how are you?" he asks in his smooth, deep voice, the people around us silenced. More so because they want to know what's about to happen. The curiosity and all.

Ryker and I haven't talked in a very long time, and I've made no secret of my feelings for him over the years. As stupid as it was, I was out there like a billboard sign, just waiting for him. Since they all know what happened to me a few months ago, this is like a soap opera ready to happen. Drama … go!

"Good," I lie. "Thanks for asking." I turn my gaze back to my family at the table. They're now watching Ryker and not giving me an out. I exhale deeply.

"I've been callin' you." He sits down on the bench in front of me.

He has ... many times. Texts too. I've ignored every one of them. There's no reason now to pretend that we'll ever be together. He's made it clear over the years that it isn't going to happen. It just took JK hurting me twice for it to sink in my head, and now that it has, that dream is a puff of smoke.

"Whelp, I've got shit to do," Cooper says, standing up and pulling Bristyl with him.

"Me, too," Deke adds in, doing the same with Rylie.

Not moments later, the rest of my family leaves me sitting across from the man I crushed on for years, the man who never knew I was alive. He never saw me and only now seems to. It sucks because it's too late.

Better to get this out of the way now than wait.

"It's cool you called to make sure I'm okay. I'm good, Ryker; you don't need to call anymore."

He reaches over and grabs my hands, but I pull them away quickly. "Austyn." My name comes out like a plea.

I rise, needing to get the hell out of there. I've waited forever to hear my name on his lips like that. Wanted it more than anything. Dreamed of it since I knew what that tone meant from a man. Hearing it now is a slice to my soul.

"I have to go."

I move around the table, but don't get far before he is standing in front of me, blocking me. I have to look up due to his height.

He's gorgeous. His beard lining those delectable lips. Damn. It's another reminder of what I will never have.

"Please. Let's go talk." His eyes plead with me in only a way Ryker can do. The fun spirit isn't there, only all this seriousness that is unlike him.

"No. There's nothing to talk about. I told you I'm fine. Thanks for helping find me. I gotta go."

He captures my arms, sizzling my skin with his touch. "Baby, don't do this."

"Ryker, I'm not your baby," I whisper as he leans down and captures my lips.

I find myself kissing him back, allowing him entry into my mouth. As his tongue sweeps in, I taste the mix of tobacco and tar on him. It's not the sweet of a cigar, or the tart of chewing tobacco, but rather the salty, bitter linger of a cigarette. He steals my breath as desire and disgust of him bringing another woman here intertwine.

It's the best first kiss a woman could ask for, and when he pulls away, it takes everything in me not to burst into tears, knowing it will also be the last.

Without words, I run to my car so I can get the hell out of there.

Sometimes, everything we want isn't what we need. Facing a new reality isn't easy.

CHAPTER SIX

RYKER

She runs away from me, but not before I see the desire mixed with pain in her eyes. Not wasting a second, I dart after her, through the crowd, taking the same path as her. She reaches her car first, fumbling in her purse for her keys, but I get there before she finds them.

"Austyn," I call out, but it's like she's made it her mission to find the keys and ignores me. Using my index finger, I place it under her chin and lift her head until our eyes connect. Fear radiates in them, yet her shoulders are straight, challenging me.

It's something I love about Austyn—her strength that oozes out of her. Sometimes, I wonder if she even knows it's there. She may have been knocked down, but she's up and moving. That's her.

"I can't do this," she says softly, looking at me like she can see right through me. Like she can see all the fuck-ups in my life and all the way down to the core of me. It's how she's always looked at me, and it scares the shit out of me. No one else has ever been able to do that or make me feel that burn.

She was only nine, I believe, when I joined the club at nineteen, but none of this started then. It wasn't until around her sixteenth birthday when I, along with every other man on the planet, noticed her.

It was sick. It made me feel like the slimeball that is my father. I fought it, pushing it down. No matter how she looked at me, I kept it in the no-go zone and continued to do that for years. Then her getting hurt tweaked something inside me. Made me want and crave and desire in a way I never thought possible. Suddenly, all the things holding me back didn't seem the same. Protecting and taking care of her suddenly became top priority.

Now, judging from her expression, she looks as if she's closed that door on us. It'll be my job to open it back up.

Thinking back to what Green said, work will need to be seriously done.

"We're just talking, Austyn."

"You just kissed me!" Fire breathes life into her, and her cheeks warm.

My cock instantly gets hard, and I have to will him down.

Reaching out, I grasp the side of her face, swiping my thumb over her bottom lip. Thoughts arise of what they will look like after my cock is deep inside them or when I've kissed her so much they're swollen.

"Do it again in a heartbeat." The truth flows from my lips. There is no other way with me. I say what I mean and mean what I say; that's how it's always been, and there is no reason to have qualms about that.

"That's not just talking."

She's right, and if I don't calm my shit, she's going to leave and do it fast.

Taking a step back, I tell her, "You're right. Let's talk. No more lips involved."

Her shoulders droop just enough to show me her disappointment, then rise again.

I love all her small tells. When she's nervous, she picks at the skin around her thumb. When she's excited, her little dimple that, if you don't know it's there, you'd miss it, makes its appearance. Needless to say, I may not have been going for her, but my eyes were watching. The reason I waited is still up in the air, because I have no fucking clue. I told myself it's because of my past. Only, the more I look in the mirror at the man I am today, the more I know nothing of my history touches me.

"There isn't anything to talk about, Ryker."

Placing my hands in my pockets, giving off a relaxed vibe, I say, "I just want to know how you're really doing. None of that 'good' bullshit because, when you looked left while saying it, I could tell you were lying."

When she gasps, I smile inside. She thinks I don't know her, but I do. Maybe even better than herself.

"I wasn't lying." As her eyes dart left, she catches herself. This time, the chuckle escapes me.

"Right. Let's just sit in your car and talk. No pressure."

Her eyes narrow and her face reddens. "You think you know me, but I've got news for you—you don't know shit."

"Calm down, woman." I place my hands on her shoulders, getting closer to her, and her body stills at my touch like it's affecting her in some way.

Something in my gut tells me that I need to go slow with Austyn.

Not only is it what happened with JK, but there is something else she's skittish about. I make a decision, following what Green told me.

"We're friends. Been friends for a long fuckin' time. This is just two friends catching up."

She huffs out a breath, and just as I'm about to take it as my cue, she says, "Fine. Ten minutes." Her body gives her away, but her eyes show her fight against this, against me.

Challenge accepted.

My smile is wide. I should kiss her again, but I don't.

Slow. Fuck, I've never done slow once in my whole damn life, yet here I am, trying it with Austyn. The one who actually matters. The one I give a shit about.

Sliding into the passenger seat, I see her grip the steering wheel so tight her knuckles are stretched white. It's hot, just like all the other things she does that makes her that way.

"Rumor is you got your own place." Starting off light is the only choice. Jumping in with I-want-you-under-me-now is crossing the friend line, something she's not ready for.

Her chest decompresses as she continues to look out the window, making it a point not to give me her attention. That's alright; we can play this.

"Yeah. Emery and I got an apartment."

She makes it seem so hard to talk to me, which I don't quite understand, considering she used to talk my ear off all the time. I don't like this change in her.

"And workin' again at that hair place?"

This time, her eyes come to me, fire breathing out of them. If she were a dragon, I'd be scorched. "Don't you need to get back to your date?" The last word is clipped and tight. She's jealous. At least that's a start in the right direction.

"No date, Austyn."

Her head jerks and a curl comes to her lips. "I can't believe you came here with her then kissed me. Do you know how gross that is?"

I must admit, I'm loving her jealousness. Tells me she cares. That she gives a fuck. What I don't want it to do is hurt her.

"She's my cousin, and that's some sick shit, Austyn."

"Oh, so you *do* have standards," she snaps, then turns back to the window.

I should feel a twinge of guilt for that, but I don't. It's my life and I live it the way I want. I want pussy, I get pussy. I want to ride, I ride. That's how it is when you come from a household that has so much control over you that you can't piss without someone knowing exactly where you are and the approximate time you'll be back.

Control is all I have.

I laugh it off, hanging my arm out the window. "Yep. Even little ol' me has standards. They aren't the best, but I still got 'em."

"You're an asshole," she grunts out, crossing her arms over her chest and pushing up her pert tits.

Damn, they're beautiful. Images of my cock running between them come to mind, making my cock harden, pressing against the zipper of my jeans. *Fuck.*

"I know. Been called worse." I huff out a breath and leave the joking aside for a moment, getting serious. "You've known me for years, and I get your assessment of me. I've never done anything to prove you wrong. Women come and women go, but not fuckin' one has stayed."

"Couldn't get your hooks in her, huh?" A small smirk plays on her lips like she thinks she one-upped me. *Too bad.*

"More like I didn't want my hooks in any of them. They weren't fuckin' worth it."

Her eyes meet mine, her mouth going a bit slack. It only lasts a moment before she looks at the clock. "Oh, look, it's been ten minutes. You need to go."

Ignoring her, I ask, "How are you really? Are you sleeping?"

Austyn closes her eyes, giving me the answer. She doesn't sleep much. She's thinking about what happened. *Fuck.*

Her head falls to the headrest. "Some."

"So, not really."

"Depends on the night."

I hate that she has this. Hate that I'm not there to help her through those nights, something else she's not ready for yet. It's on me to figure out how to change that.

"Eating?"

"What is this, four thousand questions?" she clips, irritation dripping from each word.

"I've only asked you three, Austyn."

The tension in the car is thick. Not only with the lust that I have for this woman, but from her anger, frustration, and fear. It's all there, plain as day, like all her cards are laid out on the table.

She huffs out, "Right. Some."

Which means she isn't eating as much as she should. Fucking woman.

"You have to take care of yourself."

"Yeah, I do. Now please go, *friend.*" Friend is said as a challenge. One that is fully accepted and will be succeeded.

"You got it." I rest my hand on the door latch. "You need anything, Austyn, you call me. No hesitations, no questions asked, I'll be there." Without another word, I exit the car.

She sits there for a few moments before firing up the car and darting out of the lot.

Feet apart, I rub my hand over my face. Fuck, this woman is going to put me through the wringer. The thing is, I know coming out on the other side will be worth it. Every fucking moment will be worth it. Therefore, I'll do this friend shit and get her past all the demons, or do my damnedest to try.

Pulling out my smokes, I tap one out and light it with my Zippo, inhaling the tar that will coat my lungs as I make my way back to the group of partiers.

I feel the burn in my lungs. My heart pulses inside my chest, craving more of her.

All in due time, Austyn.

CHAPTER SEVEN

Austyn

Hands hold me down, three sets of them. Whatever they gave me makes it easy for them to control my movements. I'm weaker.

I cry out as the man stands above my naked body and thrusts hard into me, breaking the barrier I held intact for twenty years.

"Fuck yeah. Virgin pussy, my favorite," he grunts as tears fall from my eyes and pain courses through my body. Each movement hurts more than the next, like he's tearing me from the inside out.

"Please stop." My words are slurred and difficult to understand.

The man just laughs as the other men pull me harder, stretching me out and yanking at my muscles.

More cries of pain. More laughter.

Laughter.

Laughter.

I bolt upright in the bed, sweat coating my skin, my breathing erratic. The room is mine, not his. Mine. Only with that realization does my breathing catch and I'm able to take some deep breaths.

I reach over and turn on the lamp that sits on my nightstand, illuminating the space. My dresser is on one wall with the mirror hanging on the back of the closet door. My clothes are everywhere, and boxes line the room. Yes, my room.

I push all negative thoughts from my head.

The problem is, looking up JK on the flash drive and finding out more about him, it opened it all back up. The helplessness, the hurt, the anger—all of it bubbles to the surface.

That man took two things from me that I can never get back, and he must pay for it. He *will* pay for it.

He got away last time, when he sliced at my body, making me bleed and enjoying it like the sick, twisted fuck he is. The world needs to be rid of filth like him. *I* need to be rid of him. He needs to know what it feels like to bleed, inside and out.

After a shower where I tried to rid the dirt and dream from me, I pull open my laptop and scroll through the information again. There isn't a lot to go on, which sucks, but there are some offshore accounts that I can suspend so he can't get any money from them. Then, with a few clicks, I alter each account so the money spins around in cyberspace, jumping from bank to bank and making it so it dumps into an account for me. I'll call it restitution. It's the least he can do for me. Even his millions won't fix all the damage he's done, but maybe it'll weed him out.

Adding a few worms to the email addresses he uses most is about the best I have so far, because I needed a break and fell asleep.

The brothers have been looking hard for him, but they have come up shy each time they get close, at least according to the notes Buzz has in the system. There are details of where JK was and at what times. Then how the club thinks he slipped away. They are trying to track a pattern, and their notes are meticulous.

As a knock comes to the door, I shut the laptop and open the door.

My father is standing on the other side. Emery must have let him into the apartment.

"Hey, Dad."

He walks in, turns to me, and crosses his arms. This is the pose for when I've done something I shouldn't have. Fear spikes that he figured out about me going into the computers. I don't see how, though, considering I put everything back the way it's supposed to be. He's so damn smart; I wouldn't put it past him to know. *Shit.*

"Care to tell me what that scene with Ryker was about?"

Part of me is relieved. Not that I want to talk about Ryker, but it's better than the computers.

"Nothing. There's nothing."

"Bullshit. Don't play games with me. Ryker isn't a man who will accept that."

Anger spikes, but I control it. "Thought you didn't get involved in shit like this."

"If it involves you, then yeah, I get involved." He moves closer to me. "You've changed since that shit happened to you, and I don't know what to do to help."

I have in more ways than one. Some things will never be the same. I don't think I'll ever be back to the me before all this went down. That doesn't mean I'm not a survivor. That's what my parents taught me— how to fuckin' survive.

"We all change, Dad. It's part of growing up and becoming your own person."

He steps closer. "Not like this. Not changin' who you are and becomin' somethin' you're not."

My dad and I are close. There were times when he was so protective it felt suffocating. Then there were other times when I wished anything for him to be with me, yet he'd given me space.

He's always said we need to spread our wings and fly, but it doesn't mean he has to like it. With my brothers, it's different. I know it. They know it. He knows it. I accepted it a long time ago.

It kills me that he sees it. That he knows what happened to me. That he lives with that. Lives with the thought that he didn't protect me. He did, though. He gave me strength.

He blows out a deep breath, stepping away from me and moving toward the door. Then he stops with his hand on the handle. "Ryker comes off snarky with quips, but there's more to the man than meets the eye. His loyalty runs deep, and he's not a man to let go of something he wants."

"Dad, you playin' matchmaker?" I tease.

"Nah, just want you to know what you've got in store." He winks.

"Don't. Ryker was a childhood crush and nothing more." At least, not now. Not ever. I could tell him that Ryker wants to be friends now, but there's no point in that, either.

"Keep tellin' yourself that." He says no more, leaving the room and shutting the door behind him.

I move to let him out, but then I hear the front door shut and don't bother. He's locked it; I know it.

Ryker, I remember when he first started prospecting for the Ravage

MC and coming around. The first moment I saw him, my world stopped and tilted on its axis. Something inside me changed. Even young, I felt it. I just didn't know exactly what it was at the time. He's ten years older than me, and I was only eight when he prospected, and nine when he joined.

Never. Not once did he ever show any interest in me, other than his brother's kid or younger sister. He'd rub the top of my head jokingly, and I hated it. Even when I turned eighteen, nothing but more of the same, each time more irritating than the last.

I spent years making it no secret I wanted him, but he never wanted me. I got it. And it took a life-changing event to put that in perspective.

Now he's suddenly taking interest. Like I'm a challenge or something, which is so far from the case it's actually funny. If he knew everything, he wouldn't want anything to do with me. It's better this way. He wants to be friends, but I'm not even sure how to do that with him. I know spending time with him isn't a good thing.

The ways he looked at me in my car. His pointed, no-holds-barred words. His body language and the way he held back from touching me when I knew he wanted to. He'll be a diversion I don't need right now. My mission isn't Ryker. It's JK.

I sit up, needing to get my mind off Ryker, and flip open the laptop. I click on a file, and my stomach bottoms out.

Pictures of the compound I was held in and hurt pop up. JK's smiling face is in several of them. My gut squeezes so tightly vomit threatens to come out.

My eyesight is hazy, like there is a fog over it. I'm unable to see ten feet in front of me, though sounds of movement are all around me, along with murmurs from a stern voice.

That voice.

I remember it.

I hear it in my nightmares. The ones that were only tamed when Deke stayed at my house.

I desperately have to get out of here, far away from him. However, my arms feel like hundred-pound weights, yet light at the same time. I go to move them, but they don't budge. It's the same story with my legs and torso.

Blinking, I try to make sense of where I am and what exactly is going on.

When I left my apartment, I looked everywhere around me before exiting. I didn't expect a Taser to come shooting from a distance and knock me on my ass. He injected me with something, probably the same thing as last time, the same thing that made my limbs go weak, then my mind.

Last time …

Panic fills me at just the thought, as the memories bombard me, ones I want to forget and move past.

This doesn't bode well for me. I barely got away before. I didn't think I'd ever be able to stand on my own two feet again. This time will be worse. I know it.

He's evil. Beyond evil.

Cooper told me to get right to the clubhouse. He warned me the brothers would notice if I'm not there. They have to because, for once, no amount of the brute force my mother taught me is going to help. Not when my body is uncontrollable, and my brain is as high as a kite.

My head jerks from a powerful force, maybe a hand. There are no cries or tears. I don't feel the pain, only a slight sting and the movement. The drugs must be more powerful than before, because I felt everything last time. Remember everything. The brutality, the tearing, the burning—everything.

"You fucking little cunt. Get rid of my baby, now I get rid of you."

Fear slices through me. I try to move my arms and legs, but it's no use.

He pulls my hair so hard my neck angles down in an unnatural way. Again, no pain, only pressure.

"Know it was mine. The other three, I made them use condoms. Not me. When I pushed through that virgin barrier, I wanted you filled with only me. Wanted you to remember who you belonged to. Then I find out you killed my baby!" The pressure becomes more. Now I do cry out. "Had my guys track you and found you after you murdered my baby! Bitch, you're going to pay … in every fucking way possible."

Bile rises up my throat, burning as I try to push it down. This man hurt me in more ways than just physical, and I hate him. Hate what he and his men did to me. I can still feel the pain of when he took me. Can still feel the guys holding me down by my arms and legs while I screamed out, trying to fight back. Every damn detail of what he did to me is etched on my soul for eternity.

My baby. I fight back the tears at thinking of the life that grew inside me for such a short time.

Pain spears through my heart. The emptiness I feel in my stomach grows.

Innocent. I can't fight the tears as one falls out of the corner of my eye and rolls down my cheek.

A sharp pain comes to my side, and then wetness falls from my body.

"Shouldn't have given you so much. Want you to feel this."

"Please don't, JK," I whisper, just as another slice of pain comes. Then another. And another.

It would be better if I were dead.

I'm not dead, and now I'm coming for him. Come hell or high water, he's going out.

CHAPTER EIGHT

Austyn

One.

My arms strain as I pull my weight up until my chin touches the bar, then I let my body fall back down.

Two.

Repeat. Up, knees bent and ankles crossed. Down.

Three.

Over and over.

The repetitions continue, sweat pouring from my face, down my chest, and to the floor below me. Regulating my breathing, I work to fight the quivering now coming from my muscles that want me to stop, urging me to take a break.

There is no break. There is no stopping, not until I feel I've had enough.

My body can handle more, so I push, moving on to crunches, then twisting my body, my abs feeling each movement.

"Austyn," Charlie calls from the mat in front of me.

Charlie's an older man, but I bet he could still kick my ass if he wanted to. The man has moves. I've seen him in the ring before, sparring. He's owned this gym for as long as I can remember and takes a special interest in those who visit his establishment. Good for him, not so good when you don't want to talk, just workout until your body can't anymore.

I should've gone to the clubhouse and worked out where my mom taught me years ago, but I needed different scenery. This is what I get for that.

When my feet hit the mat, I rub my hands down my short spandex workout shorts. They are red hot and more than likely have a few blisters. It's always the sign I've done my work here.

"Charlie."

"Good to see ya here." He smiles as I walk over, grab my towel, and wipe the sweat off my face and neck.

"Nice change of pace."

His face grows serious. I know what's coming. Even though I hate it, I refuse to be a bitch to him.

"How ya holdin' up?" And *boom*.

Placing the towel around my neck, I tell him, "Good. Every day's getting better."

"You need anything, you let me know."

I must admit, I'm surprised that he dropped it so quickly. Most people would go in for the kill when they have me to themselves. Not Charlie. I respect that.

"Will do." It's time to get the hell out of here.

Walking out of the gym, I'm alert as I take in my surroundings just to be safe. What I'm not expecting to find is Ryker standing against the door of my car, arms and ankles crossed in front of him, sexy as hell, with his eyes on me.

Hiking my workout bag up my shoulder, I make my way toward him.

"What do I owe this honor?" I tease to lighten the mood. Considering our car conversation and him wanting to be friends, this is how I decided to play it when we saw each other again. I'd be me, but a knowing me. A controlled me. A me who won't let her feelings get involved in any way, shape, or form. A me who has her eye on the prize.

He shrugs. "I got the short straw."

"Huh?" I have no idea what he's talking about.

"Bodyguard duty. But then Cruz told me it was *your* body I was guarding, and I was all over it." His eyes grow dark with desire in a way I used to dream about. "The straw suddenly didn't seem so short."

While I do like that I have the joking, teasing Ryker back, what he says doesn't make me happy.

I stand in front of him, wanting to roll my eyes but refrain. "Bet you say that to all the girls."

Ryker shifts, standing to his full height, which luckily blocks the sunlight from my eyes, but unluckily makes me have to look up at him. His glasses shine in the sunlight while his muscled, tattooed arms bulge out of his black T-shirt. His jeans fit him as if they were custom-made, hanging low on his hips. All of it is hot. Too hot. *Shit.*

"What the hell is bodyguard duty?"

"You and me, we're a team now."

I blink rapidly as my chest constricts, trying to process what he's saying. No, this wasn't part of the deal. Ryker can't follow me around all the time. That'll be the same as if I lived at home, which is why I left.

"You're shitting me."

His gorgeous smile appears, lighting up his entire face. "Nope. Where you go, I go."

"Don't you have a job?" He works at Banner Automotive with the rest of the guys and has club stuff. He doesn't have time to babysit me.

He moves his head just a touch. "You're my job now."

This can't be happening.

I pull out my phone and dial my father's number. He answers on the second ring.

"What's this about Ryker being my bodyguard, Dad?"

When his deep laugh comes across the phone, my grip on the phone gets tighter, causing the plastic to groan.

"Said you could move out on your own. I didn't say you wouldn't be watched."

"This is ridiculous." I turn from Ryker and bite the side of my thumb. "He can't be around me all the time, Dad."

"It's either that or you go on lockdown. Don't give a fuck what you pick; choice is yours. But I'm not fuckin' around, Austyn. You will be safe. You will be protected. You will have someone at your back at all times." The way he firmly says each word has me paying attention. This is something he won't budge on.

"And that has to be Ryker?"

"He told me you two were friends now."

I spin around and pin Ryker with my eyes. He says nothing, not even moving. *Jerk.*

"This shouldn't be a problem, then," my father continues. "He's Ravage. We're family. He will protect you." A pause, then a bomb drop. "Austyn, you should know, he needs to stay at your place with you."

"No. That's not happening."

There's not even a split-second of hesitation before he replies, "Then lockdown." My father will do it in a heartbeat too. Hell, he'll come right now where I'm standing, pick me up on his bike, and take me to the clubhouse himself. He's putting me between a rock and a hard place. *Shit.*

Ryker can't stay with Emery and I. That wasn't in the plan.

"Do you really think it's a good idea for him to stay with us? Why doesn't he just go home at the end of the night?"

He scoffs. "At least you've warmed up to the idea of him being your bodyguard quickly. But no. Shit happens in the night, and I need someone there."

"You've got to be kidding me."

"Nope. You wanted your freedom, to get back to life. You've made your decision, baby girl. Live with it. Bye." The phone line goes dead. I pull it from my ear and place it in my pocket.

This isn't happening. How am I going to go after JK if I have someone watching my every move? There's no way.

"So, where we goin' next?" Ryker asks.

I look for his truck or bike, but nothing is around. He had someone drop him off. *Great.*

"Home to shower."

He touches my arm, sending zaps of electricity through my body. "You need help getting all soaped up, you let me know." He winks before moving around to the side of the car and getting in.

My body flushes.

Friends, my ass.

"What's going on?" Emery asks, setting her keys down on the table as she eyes Ryker, who is lounging on our couch, bag of chips beside him and a remote in his hand.

The afternoon hasn't been bad, considering I spent much of the time in my bedroom, but I can't spend my life in there.

"We have a roommate."

Emery coughs. "What?"

"I'm her bodyguard," Ryker says through a mouthful of chips. At least he chewed them first. "That body is mine to guard."

I roll my eyes to the ceiling.

"Wait, Ryker is your bodyguard and staying here, with us? For how long?"

Ryker beats me to answer, which is good because I have no idea. "Until that dickhead is caught."

Fuck.

"This is going to be interesting," Emery says, giving me a holy-fucking-shit look. "What's for dinner? It smells good."

Stirring the pot of sauce, I look up from it to see that the question has piqued Ryker's interest too. "Just pasta, hamburger, sauce, and cheese."

"Oh, my gawd! I love that! I haven't had it in forever," Emery says excitedly, turning toward Ryker and continuing. "You eat this, you'll want to marry her."

She did not just say that. Did she just say that? I'm going to kill her. I am. *Holy shit.*

Ryker chuckles. "Let me be the judge of that."

There are so many things I could say here. I could balk and make a point that, that is never going to happen. Or I could tell him that he's not eating with us so it doesn't matter. Or I could just call him a jackass and be done with it. I do none of those things.

If I do, it will egg him on, and my energy is too depleted to argue with him. I want to eat and go to my room, where I can get back on my computer.

The food smells great as I put the finishing touches on it, then put it on plates. "Come and get it."

Ryker winks at me before grabbing his plate and going to the table. This is going to be a long-ass night.

Before I can find my escape, Ryker scoops his first bite. His eyes lock on mine as the appreciation for a good meal shows and so much more.

My heart beats so hard in my chest I can hear the roaring in my ears.

There is no more.

No, the only thing I have room for inside me is retribution. Ryker can't happen.

CHAPTER NINE

RYKER

Fuck, every fucking time she rolls her eyes to the ceiling, I want to grab her, pull her to me, and devour her lips. But watching her today, really watching her, she has more hesitation in her than I initially thought. JK did a number on her, which only pisses me off more where he's concerned. She shouldn't have any of that clouding her mind, yet she does. And from the looks of it, it's often.

"Here." Austyn hands me a pillow and blanket. The clock says it's still early, but I've thrown her a curveball and am going to let her ride this play. The way she cooked dinner, only to scurry to her room, lets me know she is off-balance having me here. She needs space.

I reach out and take them. "Thanks."

She turns on her heels. "Night." Seconds later, I hear the door to her room clicking shut.

Emery left, so it's just Austyn and I in this small space. My cock grows hard as I toss everything onto the couch.

Friends. What the fuck was I thinking?

"You don't have to come," Austyn says from the door, a large bag hanging off her shoulder.

"Nothing more I'd like to do than hang out at a fuckin' hair place."

She laughs. I love the damn sound of it. It was missed for so long. I'd do whatever is needed to keep it.

"Sure. Maybe you can get in the chair and I'll give you some highlights."

"Hell no."

She laughs harder, and I suck it in, inhaling it like a drug. Like a concoction I never want to go away. It's heady and intoxicating.

She reaches up high and runs her fingers through my hair, sending a shock from my scalp to my fucking boots. "It could use a trim."

My breathing comes quicker. This holding back shit is harder than I ever thought it would be. It's driving me crazy that I can't just pull her to me and take what I want.

She removes her hand, taking the sensations with her. "Come on; I don't want to be late."

"Just think, we get to do that all again tomorrow." Austyn throws her head back to the passenger side headrest, happiness radiating off her in waves.

She loves her job. Full-out loves it. She talks with the people there like she's known them for years. It may all be superficial shit that doesn't get to the core of who she is, but that doesn't matter. How she deals with so many people all the time is admirable. There's no way in hell I'd be able to do that shit.

"That blue-haired bitty needed to get laid."

Her laugh fills the car. "Yeah, she's been widowed for years and always has something to say. When she told you all that ink made you look like a road map, I died. Then you told her it was a window to your soul." Tears stream from her eyes as she continues to laugh loudly.

"They are."

She brings her hand to her chest, holding it there. "You're too much."

"Nah, just the right enough of much."

She shakes her head. "You have any plans tonight?"

On a shrug, I answer, "Depends on what you're doin'."

"Emery has something with her mom, so do you want to pick up some food and just hang out?"

"Let me guess, you want Chinese."

Her head whips toward me. "How did you know that?"

"You want Hawaiian chicken, fried rice, and egg rolls."

She gapes at me. It brings me satisfaction that she doesn't think I know her. How wrong she is.

My attention has been on her for years. I remember everything, and some things she probably doesn't want me to know. I don't give a shit.

"Holy shit," she breathes out in this sexy way that has my cock reacting. "How do you know that?"

Turning toward her, I tip my lip up in a smirk. "I know what's important."

81

She moves, focusing her attention out the windshield.

I'll make her see ... eventually.

We get the Chinese. We eat the Chinese. She's quiet during dinner, and when I suggest we watch a movie and pick one with The Rock in it, her eyes widen in shock once more. She's loved his movies forever, it seems.

That leads us to me on one side of the couch, lying down, and her on the other side, both watching the movie. In the same space, together, but not.

My hand itches to grab her. Instead, I pull her feet toward me. She tries to pull away, but I hold strong.

"What are you doing?"

"Relax, Austyn. You've been on them all day." With pressure, I massage her feet, rubbing small circles with my thumbs and pushing into the parts she needs it. I watch for her cues, and when she gives me those throaty moans or groans, I make sure to do those spots over and over.

The tension in her body leaves, and then she relaxes into my touch. I pay attention to both feet, rubbing and kneading. We stay like this for a long time, until her eyes close and she falls fast asleep.

Fuck, this shit is harder than I thought.

Friends.

I'm a dumbass.

It only drives home the point that I need to find JK and eliminate him. Austyn is mine, and no one touches what's mine. He will pay for what he did to her.

As I carefully lift her from the couch, she plasters herself to my body, one hand gripping my shirt. I take a moment to enjoy the feel, searing it in my memories.

I move her to the bed and lay her down. Her dark hair fans out across the pillow. She looks beautiful as hell. I lean down and brush a kiss against her lips, then cover her up and leave the room.

Making my way to the living room, the urge to smoke hits. The balcony is right off the dining room area. I've been taking full advantage of it. Austyn even put a chair out there for me to sit on.

As I sit, light, and inhale, my thoughts are all jumbled. Between Austyn, finding JK, and my family, everything is a fucking mess right now.

All I can do is roll with it.

CHAPTER TEN

Austyn

I slam my computer closed and flop back onto my bed with a *whoosh*. The money is still bouncing everywhere. Luckily, it's moving so fast the worm I put with it is making it difficult for others to track. The worm for the emails hasn't done a damn thing since JK hasn't checked it. In order for it to work, he needs to reply to the damn things. I added one that will give me IP addresses from the location he checks in, as well.

I could reply to the emails myself to see what the responses would be, but the less I put myself out there, the better. I want to find him, not the other way around. It's a tricky thing. One I didn't realize was so hard, surprisingly. This sneaking and stealth work is aggravating because it takes time.

Buzz taught me how to tap into feeds from security cameras. I watched around JK's mother's house from a camera on a light pole down the road from her place, but I never saw him. It would be the place people will most likely look for him, so if he's smart, he'll stay far away.

Every end is coming up dead, and I'm really feeling for my father and the brothers. If this is what it feels like to have your hands tied and do nothing, they can have that shit back.

A cough comes from the living room, and I roll into my pillow with a groan.

Ryker.

For a little over a week now, he's been by my side everywhere I go. We've had to go to the clubhouse a couple of times so he can attend meetings with the brothers and stop by his place for clothes. Other than that, he's been stuck to me like glue.

Months ago, I'd have been eating this up, having him so near to me. The way he touches me, rubs my feet to soothe out the aches. Years I've wanted this. Years.

Ryker has always been there. Always been the one who was so close yet so damn far away. Elusive when it came to me. There, but not.

A brush of a hand here or there or a ruffle of the hair was about the only physical contact we've ever had. I wanted more. So much more with him, but it wasn't in the cards.

Prom was the worst. My father made me have my date, Shawn, meet me at the clubhouse instead of our house. My father had all the brothers outside, waiting for him with the sole purpose of scaring the shit of him, which they did. I was surprised we didn't have to stop so he could change his pants from pissing himself.

As my mother and grandma took pictures of us, my gaze continually landed on Ryker. His strong arms crossed over his chest, breathing in and out heavily, his eyes narrowed, checking the guy out. He stood so tall and powerful. He didn't even have to come close to me for me to feel it. It was like a punch to the stomach that sent chills throughout my body.

I'd wished and hoped that Ryker would be the one standing next to me instead of Shawn. Imagined Ryker in his jeans, black T-shirt and cut, taking me to prom where we'd dance the night away and hang out. Needless to say, that was stupid. I can't see Ryker doing the dancing thing. Hope is a powerful thing.

Even when Shawn and I left, I watched Ryker as his eyes never left the car.

All I wanted was for Ryker to take my hand and lead me wherever he wanted me to go, but that didn't happen.

Now, he's living with me. On the couch. In my apartment. I see him every freaking day. My old self would love this. Relish in it and hook him with everything I had inside me.

Unfortunately, life has a way of screwing people, of twisting plans and making them unreachable, unattainable, and crushing at the same time. It throws what you desperately want in your face like splattered mud. Yet, you still can't have it. Even with him here, in my space, protecting me, I can't.

It's all because of one man who decided I was an easy target one night and went in for the kill. He tore me from the inside out, making me damaged, used, and disgusting. To this day, the shower still doesn't clean the filth he put all over me. It doesn't erase the phantom feelings I get from time to time. It doesn't clean me. Nothing will clean me and take me back to my old self.

I rub my belly as the emptiness inside consumes me like it does every other time I think of my baby. The one *he* gave me that I couldn't keep.

It's a mixed place to be—this piece of you created with a monster—and a hell you can't imagine ever surviving again. There is still a longing inside me, though turning back time isn't an option. Even if I could change things, how? There isn't anything that could've been different in my eyes. I just know there is this piece of me, no matter the circumstances of its conception, that's dark and empty, devoid of life. It eats at me every moment, every breath, feeding and growing.

I groan, wiping the thoughts from my mind, just as there's another noise from the living room.

Looking at the clock, I see it's only ten-thirty. Going to my room for alone time has been my regimen, but this is getting ridiculous.

Pulling off the covers and clambering out of bed in my pajama shorts and oversized T-shirt that I stole from Nox a while back, I make my way to the living room. The sounds of the television filter through the hallway as gunshots echo and words are said that can't be made out.

Ryker lies on the couch, his boots on the floor in front of him, his feet up on the cushions. His arms are behind his head, and his focus is on the TV.

As if he can sense me, he turns and our gazes lock. My pulse spikes as the hairs on my arms prickle at the fierceness of his look. We're lost in each other for a brief moment in time, and it's glorious.

I give a slight cough, breaking the connection, and turn toward the kitchen. "I'm hungry. You want anything?"

I hear rustling and know he's getting up from the couch. His pattered footsteps tell me he's coming my way.

Sucking in a breath, the refrigerator jingles from the condiments on the door as I open it. Nothing looks good to me. Left over spaghetti, Chinese, cheese—blah.

His stare is on me. I feel it zapping me in the back, and my body begins to heat. Ignoring this, I check out the freezer and, low and behold, mint chocolate chip ice cream. *Ding! Ding! Ding! We have a winner.*

"I'll take some of that," he says, leaning his shoulder against the doorjamb.

It takes everything I have not to allow my jaw to drop to the floor. He's wearing basketball shorts that ride low on his hips and a tank top that's showing all his muscles and tattoos. Going to bed early means I've been missing out on this view for the past week and a half. *Shit.*

Tearing my eyes away, I open the drawer and pull out two spoons, then point them toward the couch. His soft chuckle fills the space as he moves, sitting on the right side of the couch. I move to the left, pull the top off the ice cream, and then hand him a spoon.

"What are you watching?" I dig into the ice cream then take a bite. The taste of mint explodes on my lips. Holding back a moan is difficult.

"*Die Hard.* Nothing else looked good." He digs into the mint chocolate chip while I try to hold the carton steady for him. My arm shakes at his movements, or maybe it's just being this close to him.

We sit like this for a while, both watching the movie, eating and not speaking.

Why does this have to be so strange? We are *friends,* right?

I lick the spoon then hand him the rest of the container.

"I'm good."

Nodding, I take it to the kitchen and put it back in the freezer.

Taking a seat back on the couch, I ask, "Aren't you a little tired of this every night? You have a life; surely, this is imposing on it."

He stretches his arm out over the top of the couch, close to me, but not touching. "Someone's gotta guard that hot body." He winks, and part of me melts. *Damn him.*

"What about taking rotations? I know my father isn't going to let this go, and I'm resigned to that. But what if Nox, Jacks, or Green comes over for a while? That'll give you a break."

Something pulsates off Ryker. It's so powerful it pulls me. His face is controlled, but his eyes are working and doing it hard.

"No one stays here but me." The words are dangerous in a way I haven't heard from Ryker in all my years of knowing him. So much so my lips stay shut on that topic for the rest of the night.

Eventually, Ryker moves to lay down, stretching his long body across the couch.

"What are you doing?" I ask stupidly, like I can't see what he's doing nor feel his legs behind my back.

"Come here." He holds out his arms, and everything freezes in time. What's going on here? "Just rest your head on my chest. My legs are killin' me, and I need to put them up."

"Do you have problems with your legs?"

"Nope." His arms are still out, waiting for me. I let out a long yawn, and he chuckles. "Lie down."

I shouldn't, but my body isn't catching up with my brain.

As I lay my cheek on his chest, I feel how hard and muscled it is. Not knowing where to put my hand, I rest it next to my head. It sucks not having much experience in this department. One would think I could hack it, yet my nerves are fluttering in my stomach.

He places his hand on my back, moving it in slow circles. Slowly, my body softens and my eyes drift closed. This is the most comforting and relaxed I've ever felt with a man. God help me.

"Let me know when you want to go," Ryker says, leaving me outside with Emery, my mother, and Angel, who is Emery's mother, as he strides toward the clubhouse.

I won't lie. I didn't want to come. Didn't want to be at a big party where everyone would be.

I keep reminding myself that it isn't because I don't want to see Ryker with one of the club mommas. It has nothing to do with that. He has every right to do anything he wanted. So what if I fell asleep with my head on his chest, listening to the steady beat of his heart and breathing in his tobacco? That doesn't matter. He's a free man, able to do whatever he wants. Just like he's always been. Just like he needs to be.

Having him around all the time is screwing with me. My focus is totally jacked up. JK is my priority, and if Ryker ever found out what happened to me, he wouldn't want to be with me, anyway. I need to keep that in perspective, always in my head and never forget it.

"Right." Taking a seat next to my mother, she smiles brightly at me as Ryker enters the clubhouse while I do my best not to stare at his ass.

"Watchin' him awfully hard, Austyn. What's goin' on?" My mother isn't accusatory by any means, but she is curious.

At her words, I avert my attentions, pissed at myself for getting caught. Friends, right? Friends watch friends go into buildings. There's nothing creepy with that.

"Not a damn thing."

She turns fully toward me as Angel coughs in her hand. "I call bullshit."

"That's become your favorite word lately." It has. Every time I turn around, she's calling bullshit on me. Too bad most of the time it's true. She knows too much, always has.

"I call it like I see it." My mother flips her hair back over her shoulder then clasps her hands together, giving off a relaxed vibe, yet you know she's going to zing you with something. "Ryker's living with you. You've always had a thing for him. He obviously has one for you, so ..."

Closing my eyes, the intake of breath does nothing for my calmness. She doesn't know what JK did to me. How he held me down and ripped my virginity away from me, then had his buddies take their turns. She doesn't know how that spoiled and soiled me from the inside out. She doesn't know I had to get rid of the baby that came from that. All she knows is what happened when JK got me the second time and the pain that was inflicted on me.

I can't tell her that I'm tainted and no man will ever want to touch me. That I'm dirty and gross, and there's nothing that can be done about it. It's like a festering thorn deep under my skin, digging itself deeper and deeper with each moment that passes, cutting me.

I can tell my mother none of this. Therefore, she'll never really know why. No one can know. If it's talked about, then I fear that it'll never go away. Everyone will remember it every second of the day, and I'll never be able to get past or escape it. Truthfully, I don't know how to get past any of this, except to find JK and make him pay.

"Yeah, he's staying, but that's it."

When my mother's keen gaze hits me hard, I avert my eyes, not wanting her to see inside me.

"You've been in love with him since you met him. Don't tell me all that has gone away. Is this because of JK and what he did?"

I love my mother. I really, really do. But this is too close for comfort. I feel like fire ants are crawling all over my skin, biting me as they swarm, threatening to take me over. My mother is a force to be reckoned with and many won't take her on. Normally, I never would, either, but I need this to stop. I need it all to stop before those ants envelop me.

Looking her dead in the eye, I tell her, "Mom, I love you, but you need to let this go. Now."

I feel as if she's grabbing something inside me and pulling out the information she needs with her gaze. She is determined to figure out what is inside my head.

This time, I can't look away. She should know this is serious, and keeping eye contact with my mother is the only way to show her. She respects it.

It takes her a bit before she nods and breaks her binding spell. "Gotcha."

"Let's shoot tequila!" Emery calls out, and I groan.

Me and tequila have been friends for many years. We have a love-hate relationship. It goes down smooth, gets me drunk, and makes me happy. Then it tears up my insides and spews out of my body later.

Just then, Ryker comes out of the clubhouse with a very pretty brunette wrapped around his waist. Bile threatens to escape.

Slapping the table, I cheer, "Tequila it is!"

Emery smiles, my mother looks at Ryker knowingly, and Angel just continues to be her quiet self. This is going to be an interesting night.

Half the bottle is gone. Holding it up, I find there's more to be consumed.

My body feels fine. Memories have disappeared. Ryker has disappeared. Everything is quiet in my head for the moment. It's a feeling I haven't had in months and months.

Sure, there's a shit-ton of noise around me, but as I lean on the bar, head resting on my elbow, a calm washes over me. This leads me to taking a couple more shots and Emery following me.

"Whaaadddaa doin'?" Emery is drunk. Big time.

I take a slug from the bottle, not feeling any bit of the burn anymore. It almost tastes like water, and that's when you know you've drunk too much.

"Drinkinnnn'."

She gives me the wide-eye look. The one that says *duh, not what I'm asking*. "With Ryyyyker."

Not this again.

My mind swims, and it takes me a moment to think. Leave it to Emery to make me try to organize a complete thought on tequila.

"Nothinnnn'," is the best I can come up with. Lame, but real.

"Whatttteverr. Don't tell ya bestestttt frieeeend."

A laugh escapes me. I say nothing, just watch my best friend turn fuzzy in my vision.

The bottle is wrenched from my hand.

"Hey!"

Ryker stands there with a glare to end all glares, shaking the bottle.

"You're done." He hands the bottle over to the bartender, who puts it behind the bar so we can't reach it.

I look at the bartender. "Party pooper."

He just shrugs like he doesn't give two shits.

My attention goes back to Ryker. "Fine, Daddddd."

His nostrils flare as he steps into my space. "Lotta things I am to you, Austyn, but Dad isn't one of them. Let's go." He grabs my arm, not hard but firmly, and pulls me next to him. "Emery, you comin'?"

"Nope. I'm stayin' here tonight."

"Traitor," I tell her.

She smiles, giving me a wave. "Have fun!"

I look up to Ryker. "Ya know, you can just go back to your woman friend, and I can sleep in my father's room." My words come out a bit more slurred than I want. Guess those last shots are doing me in.

"No," is all he says as he leads me to the car while I give sloppy waves to a couple of people as I'm escorted away.

He opens the door, and I climb in, resting my head against the headrest.

"Buckle up," he orders after he climbs in.

I huff. He's so acting like my father it's not even funny. Ordering me. Making me stop drinking. Being all demanding. But something in my foggy head is telling me not to call him my dad again.

Pulling the belt, I latch it after a few failed attempts because the damn thing keeps moving, or maybe it's me.

The ride home is quiet. Ryker peers over at me several times like I'm going to go *poof* in a ball of smoke and disappear like some magician on crack. I touch my body. Nope, still here. I let a chuckle.

"What's so funny?" he asks.

"I'm just imagining I'm a magician and going to go up in a puff of smoke." I throw my arms out wide. *"Poof!"*

He throws his head back and laughs deeply, a sound I do love to hear. It gets my girl bits tingling, and that is not a good thing. Drunk and Ryker, that's not a good combination.

"Yeah, we'll see how you feel in a few hours. Let's get ya some food."

He pulls into a drive-thru and orders me a greasy burger and fries that I devour. When we make it back to the apartment, he has to help me into the place because my balance is a bit off. He leads me to the couch, and I fall onto it with a groan. The burger and booze aren't working well together, mixing like a concoction of death.

Faster than I thought my body could move, I race to the bathroom, slam my knees to the tile floor, and begin to pray to the porcelain god. I knew this would happen, but this part is the hate I have with tequila. Great going down, shitty coming up.

As my hair is pulled away from my face, mortification sets in just as I throw up again, the contents of my midnight snack now gone. Dammit, and the food was supposed to soak up all the booze.

"Go away," I tell him as I cough, but he doesn't move, just gathers my hair, keeping it behind my head.

"Do what ya gotta do, Austyn. I've got ya."

God, he's got me, the words I've always wanted to come from his mouth. Why did he have to wait so long to say them?

I shake my head as another bout comes on. My stomach doesn't have much in it. Eventually, as the nausea dissipates, I fall to my ass.

When Ryker releases my hair, I feel it fall down my back. Then he moves, and I hear water running, then a cold towel is pressed to my forehead.

He crouches down in front of me with so much compassion on his face. I'm so drunk I can't stop the walls around my stiffened heart from chipping away. Another reason for me to hate tequila.

"Thank you."

"Anything for you." He gives me a wink then rises, going back to the sink where he wets another cloth before handing it to me. "For your mouth."

I gratefully take it and wipe my mouth, even sticking my tongue out and wiping it. The acidic taste still lingers, though.

"Do you think you're done?"

Not feeling any more rumbling, I answer with a, "Yeah."

With no effort at all, he leans down and picks me up from the floor, carrying me to my room. He sets me gently down on the bed then removes my shoes, tossing them to the floor. When he grabs my oversized T-shirt, my brows pinch together. *He's not going to change me, is he?*

"Up," he demands, and my arms go.

Ryker doesn't remove my bra, just pulls the large shirt over my head then unbuttons my shorts and pulls them down my legs. I instantly dampen from this act, having wanted this exact thing so many times before, and here it is, happening while I'm piss-ass drunk.

Ryker grabs the garbage can, putting it next to my bed, which is a very thoughtful and smart thing to do. He then pulls the covers over top of me, brushes his lips over my forehead, and then leaves the room. I instantly pass out.

It's the only peace I can seem to find in my head.

CHAPTER ELEVEN

RYKER

I'd lost count of the days I've spent with Austyn. We've come up with a routine. Not one that I'd like to do forever, in that she can keep her hair shit to herself, but one I can tolerate for now.

It's been five days since Austyn's drunken fest at the clubhouse. She needed to unwind, that's why I let it go on for as long as I did, but when I started seeing some of the guys from another charter giving her the eye, I moved in.

Fuck that. No one touches Austyn.

"Can you bring me the plates please?" Austyn asks with her hands in a tub of sudsy water. I do as she asks and hand them to her. "Thanks."

She looks hot as hell, and my hands itch to touch her.

After dishes, we move to the couch, where we lie down, watching some stupid as hell reality show where these assholes go into the woods naked and expect to survive. Fucking morons.

The show doesn't matter, though. Austyn is curled up beside me with my arm wrapped around her. Her eyes are almost fully closed and her breathing even. Every night she falls asleep like this. Every night. It's a step.

She thought I was with that brunette, and my dumb ass hasn't told her any differently. I should have right away. It's the second time she assumed I was with someone else.

That chick was nothing. She wanted more, but no way, not when I have Austyn. Truth, I haven't been with anyone since Austyn was attacked. It's also why my cock is so fucking hard all the time. Jacking off in the shower isn't enough.

We lay for a long time, but I change the channel because that shit isn't for me and find a chopper show.

My cell rings. It's a number I don't recognize. I take it, anyway.

"Yeah?"

"Matthew?"

Only my family calls me Matthew. I got rid of that name when they banished me from home. Matthew doesn't exist anymore, only with them.

"Who is this?"

There's a hesitation on the other end. "It's Samantha."

My body locks for a moment, then I move out from under Austyn and rise from the couch. I haven't talked to my sister Samantha since I left my mother's home when she was only eight.

"What's wrong?"

More hesitation, and then her voice is quiet. "I need to leave. Me and my two babies. We have to get out of here."

I rip my hand through my hair as I pace the living room. "Are you hurt?"

"No." The answer comes immediately. "I just can't live like this anymore. Can you come and get me?"

This is strange on so many levels, especially since I haven't talked to her in so long. Part of me wants to rip out of there and go get her, but the logical side of me needs to know this isn't a setup of some kind. Some may say the world has made me cynical. I say it's made me smart.

"How'd you get my number?"

She blows out a breath, her voice trembling when she says, "Mom. She talks about you sometimes when we're alone. She said she talks to you, so I stole her phone and wrote your number down. I've had it for a while, but ..."

"But what?"

"I just need to leave. Can you help me?"

Austyn rouses from the couch, her sleepy eyes taking notice of me. Whatever she sees has her sitting up straight.

"Yeah. Where are you?"

She gives me her address and says, "You have to be really quiet. No one can see you. My neighbors are very nosy and will call Rob."

"Right. Be there in a couple of hours."

"Thank you." She disconnects the phone as I focus on Austyn.

"Need you to get dressed and come with me."

She nods and, with not a single question, runs to her room. I hear her drawers opening and closing as I lace my boots up. She comes out moments later with black jeans, dark blue shirt, and a leather jacket. Sexy.

"Gun?"

"Absolutely." She lifts the back of her jacket. I know why she's wearing it.

We jump in the truck and take off like a shot. I'm thankful I had half a mind to bring one of my rides over here the other day. I didn't want to bring the Harley because, if someone touched it, they'd be dead. I don't have time for that shit.

Austyn is very quiet, twisting her hands in her lap as she stares out the window. She wants to ask where we're going and what we're doing, but she is holding it in like a champ.

It's not that I care if people know; it's that I don't like talking about it. I don't like exposing myself to people's ridicule or attitudes toward a cult that isn't in my beliefs. I have my opinions on it, and to me, that's all that matters. I don't give a fuck what others think. Unfortunately, a part of me does care what Austyn thinks.

"We're going to pick up my sister."

Her head whips toward me. "Sister? You have a sister?"

"I have several brothers and sisters, Austyn."

"You've never brought them around or talked about them." This is true. She sounds shocked as hell that she didn't know something about me.

Gripping the steering wheel, I huff out deeply. "That's because I don't see them. Or haven't in years."

"Why not?"

I turn my head toward her briefly. "Need you to listen to what I have to say and let me get all the way through it. I know you'll have questions. We'll deal with that shit after I'm done. But babe, I need you to listen first."

"Okay." The word comes out breathless, and my cock hardens. Fuck, it's been hard for the entire time I've spent with Austyn. This should be different while talking about my fucked-up family. With

Austyn, though, it's always the same.

"My family is fucked up. This is going to sound off the wall and crazy, so just bear with me. My mother is 'married' to a man, but she's not legally married to him. She's just with him. This man has six other 'wives'." Out of the corner of my eye, I see hers widen. "Now, I don't give a fuck about how many women he has because, if they want to put up with his ass, then so be it. Now, this is fucked up part. You still with me?"

"Yeah."

"This man, James, is also married to my mother's sister and one of her cousins."

Austyn turns her entire body toward me, bringing her knee up onto the seat, the seatbelt still across her. I have her complete and undivided attention now.

"So, that means my aunt and my second-cousin are also my step-mothers. If you look at it that way, my cousins are also my half-brothers and sisters."

"Holy shit," she whispers, covering her mouth while moving her other arm across her belly.

"Yeah. It's a fucked-up thing that I don't want any part of. But the thing is, once you're in it, you're in. James will keep you in at all costs. Getting out is difficult for some. There is so much brainwashing going on that my mother wouldn't even know her name if he didn't tell her what it is. It's a shitty spot, but it's where my mom wants to be."

Austyn remains quiet, yet her leg begins to bounce. I know she's trying to control herself from asking questions.

I continue, "The other fucked up thing is, when girls are sixteen years old, they are matched with male contenders to marry. They don't have much choice on who they marry, but most of the time, it is a cousin or half-brother of some sort, which is fucking jacked in my opinion. They don't get married until eighteen, but are considered that man's spouse right away. Samantha married our cousin, half-brother, and from what she said on the phone, they have two kids. She wants out and wants me to come get her. That's what we're doing."

Looking over to Austyn, I see her staring at me. "Ask what you want."

"This guy, James, is he your father?"

"Sperm donor, yes." I fucking hate answering this shit, but it's Austyn. I'd do anything for this woman.

"He's a polygamist, and you have a shit-ton of brothers and sisters out there that you don't know. Why is that?"

Staring out at the night sky, I watch it fade to black at the horizon, just like my situation—black, empty, unwanted. At least, that's what I felt at the time. Fourteen and being pushed out of the only home you've ever known. Now, no. I just hate opening all this shit up. It's like pulling a scab off a wound and letting it bleed all over again.

"At fourteen, I was kicked out of the family."

"No!" I can hear her outrage, showing me that she cares. Love that. Wish it wasn't for this, though.

"Yeah. I had lots of questions about what was going on and why people were marrying their families. Each question turned into another question. I was sent to camp where they try to make you think the way they do—brainwash camp—but it didn't work. When I went back home, James told me to leave, that I was no longer wanted in the family. I left."

"Where did you go?"

"Streets. It wasn't pretty. Did drugs and all that shit. Stole to eat. You name it, I did it. Survival was the only thing on my mind."

"And you did."

"Abso-fucking-lutely. No way in hell I'd let that shit get me down." It took a while. Fuck, a long while. I did it, though. I got over that rejection, learning it wasn't worth my effort or energy.

It gets quiet. Austyn is staring out the window, breathing in and out.

I reach over and place my hand on her leg. "I'm good, Austyn. All that is my past. It's just coming back to kick me in the ass, and I have to do what I can to get my family out of that life, if that's what they want. I have another sister, Breanna, who turns sixteen in a month. I've warned my mother that she is to not have any men after her, which I know will happen, anyway. I'm trying to decide what I can do to help her. She doesn't need to live a life like this."

"And your mother doesn't want to leave?"

"Austyn, she's so brainwashed she thinks James walks on water. She lives in a shithole, but it's what James provides for her and what she wants to live in. I can't force her to leave. I wouldn't, anyway. If that's how she wants to live, she's a grown adult. My siblings aren't. When Samantha married, I didn't find out about it until afterward. With Breanna, I know now."

"With Ravage at your back," she adds.

"Yes, with Ravage at my back."

She places her hand on mine that is still on her thigh and holds on to me, not releasing. Neither do I.

"And Samantha wants to get away and called you to come get her?"

"Right. Her and her two kids."

She gives my hand a squeeze. "Didn't expect this tonight."

"No shit. Me, either."

I need a smoke, but with Austyn holding one hand and the other on the wheel, it isn't an option. I'm not moving, so I suffer.

"I'm happy you found the Ravage MC to give you the family you need." Her words come out a little choked, but she pulls it together.

I don't want her crying for this. It's in the past, and there's no reason for it.

"Exactly, Austyn. I have a family. One I can depend on that depends on me. That's all that matters."

"Right."

An hour away from our destination, according to the GPS, my cell rings again with the same number as before.

"Samantha?"

She gives me a soft, "Yeah."

"We're about an hour out."

"Turn around," she demands, shocking me. "I'm not leaving. Please don't come here."

"What happened between these two phone calls?" So many scenarios run through my head, all compressing together in a heap. Is she hurt? Did he find out she was leaving? Did he threaten her?

There is movement on the other end of the phone, like she's switching ears or something. "I'm just not leaving my husband. Sorry I called you."

"What does that mean?"

"Please don't come. I won't let you in, and you'll make my neighbors curious. Rob will find out, and he can't. You'll make it worse."

"Is he going to hurt you?" The thought kills me, but it's something common in this culture and forces me to ask. It reinforces the fear and makes everyone do what they are told.

"No. Just don't come, Matthew. I'm not leaving." The phone line goes dead.

I toss it into the cup holder then bang my hands on the wheel. "Fucking hell!"

Rage boils in my blood. My grip on the wheel is so tight I'm pretty sure it's going to crack.

Taking the ramp off the highway, I see a McDonalds lit up and pull the truck in there. With my hands in my hair, I lean into the steering wheel, resting my forehead on it and trying to calm the anger.

Austyn's hand comes to my shoulder, and my body jolts at first, then relaxes at the touch.

"What's going on?"

I don't move, just talk through my arms. "She's not leaving. Doesn't want to leave her husband and is sorry she called me."

"Do you think her husband found out?"

"Fuck if I know."

"I'm so sorry." She moves her hand around in small circles, a comforting caress. It's exactly what I need right now.

"Can't make her come. I mean, I could drag her out, but it'll do no good. She'll just go back. She has to want to leave. Same thing with my mother." I'll be damned if Breanna goes through this shit.

"True."

"Will you grab my laptop and pull up the address." I almost hate the request, because her hand leaves my back, but this needs to be done. Plus, I need to get my anger in check before I do it.

"What do you want me to do?"

"You already have it up?" I turn my head to see a sexy smile playing on her sensuous lips.

"Oh yeah. Do you want the security cameras or the aerial view? Or, do you know if there is an alarm system in the house we can tap into that has cameras?"

She stuns me completely.

My mouth gapes. I have watched her for years, but never once was I clued in to her computer skills.

"You know how to do all that?"

She shrugs. "Yep. Buzz taught me a lot."

He damn well did.

"Just find out whatever you can. See if the husband is anywhere to be seen, or if the house is quiet."

I lean back in the seat and look up to the ceiling of the truck. My hopes for saving one sister crashed and burned quickly tonight. It's like a roller coaster ride, going up and down with a force I'm ready to get the fuck off of.

"All is calm. No lights. No movement outside the house. They don't have interior cameras. What do we do now?"

Huffing out a breath, realizing she said *we*, I answer, "The only thing we can do. Go home."

CHAPTER TWELVE

Austyn

My mind is spinning like a tilt-a-whirl, trying to make sense of all the information Ryker just gave me. There are so many more pieces to this puzzle than I ever imagined.

I glance over at him. He looks part pissed off and part hurt. Imagining Nox being in a situation like this and me not being able to help him would kill me, just like it's doing to Ryker now.

My hands itch to reach over to him, but his body language is closed off and the silence in the cab is deafening. If this is what he needs, though, I'll give it to him. He answered all my questions, and I'm sure I'll have tons more after this fully processes. It's just a lot to compute.

When we pull up to the apartment, Ryker blows out a deep breath. He's had one cigarette after the other on the way home, and it's done nothing to calm him.

He lets out a ragged breath. "Come on; let's get some sleep." His gruff voice holds so much disappointment. It breaks my heart in two.

When we enter, I see that Emery's door is closed, telling me she's home and asleep. Ryker locks the door and moves over to the couch. I grab his hand and pull him to my bedroom, not thinking anything but wanting to soothe his pain.

"Austyn, what are you doing?"

The click of the door shutting echoes through my room. "Get ready for bed. I'm beat."

"You want me to sleep in here?"

"Yep." I move to my closet and change into my pajamas.

I hear his boots hit the floor then his jeans. I shouldn't do this. In my mind, I know it, but in my heart, I want to be his comfort tonight and soothe his pain in the only way I know.

He crawls into bed as I turn out the light then make my way over to the bed, stretching out beside him and resting my head on his shoulder.

He wraps his arm around me. "Damn nice sleepin' in a bed. Fuckin' better havin' you by my side." He leans over and kisses the top of my head.

I don't want to think of the ramifications for this. I don't want to think at all.

"Get some sleep, Ryker. Good night."

"Night, beautiful."

My heart flutters as we fall asleep.

I wake with a start, my face plastered against a hard, bare chest.

Fear hits me until I lift my head, seeing Ryker. Only then does breathing come.

Nightmares didn't haunt me last night, which I'm eternally grateful for. They are sporadic, always lingering, and I never know exactly when they are going to hit. Luckily, last night wasn't one them.

Ryker's breathing is steady and calm. His heartbeat thumps against my hand. His body is warm and inviting. Everything that I always dreamed of is right here in my bed with me.

Just a second longer, I tell myself. A second to enjoy being in his arms and feeling his comfort. A second to remember what this feels like so I can carry it with me for the rest of my life.

All too soon, reality hits me in the face. I inch out from under Ryker's arm. He doesn't so much as move as I exit the bedroom, which is good because he needs rest.

Entering the bathroom, I do my thing, running a brush through my hair. There's noise coming from the kitchen, and as I make my way in there, I find Emery chopping up vegetables at the counter.

"Hey, sleepy," she greets.

The clock reads twelve-sixteen. I haven't slept after noon in a long damn time. "Yeah."

"Where's Ryker?"

This is what I should have thought about before my wild idea to let him sleep with me. She's going to blow this totally out of proportion and probably won't keep her mouth shut about it.

I snatch a mushroom and toss it in my mouth. "In my room, and I don't want to hear anything about it."

"Holy shit! Did you fuck him?" She beams.

She's heard all about Ryker forever, best friend code and all. She has always pushed for me to make stronger moves and get his attention more. Not sure how I could have done that, besides standing naked in front of him, but whatever. Her reaction doesn't surprise me.

"Of course not."

She aims her knife at me as a supposed threat. "What do you mean *of course not*?"

"No, Emery, I didn't have sex with him, and I'm not going to. I really don't want to talk about this." Not only that, but I won't tell Ryker's business of the actual reason he's there. If he wants Emery to know where we went last night, that's up to him. I refuse to scatter his business to everyone. I wouldn't want someone to do that to me, so no way I'd do it to him.

"That's just stupid. He's in your bed. You want this. What's the problem?"

The problem is, I'm damaged, tainted, and I don't want him to deal with it. "Nothing. It's just not happening."

She sets the knife down and brushes her long hair over her shoulder. "You're kidding me, right? Years, you've wanted him, and here he is and you know he wants it. And you're not going to do anything about it? What is going on, Austyn? You've got to talk to me."

It would feel so good to tell someone about what happened to me, just for the mere fact to get if off my chest and hear her opinion, but I can't, because it would be out there. It would be real in a way it could never go away.

"It's …"

Ryker walks into the kitchen with a large stretch, and I clamp my mouth shut. Saved by him, thank you very much.

"Later," she says pointedly then looks to Ryker. "Making omelets.

Want one?"

"Hell yeah!"

He doesn't appear to have the lasting effects from last night still on him, but I know all too well looks can be deceiving.

"Do you want to talk about it?" I ask Ryker on the way to the store, which I don't want to go, but in the words of Ryker *'I got the short straw.'* Good thing the list isn't too long. I once gave Emery a list as long as my arm. She was pissed, but I was on the rag and needed chocolate, like every kind they had.

"Nah, nothin' to say, beautiful. Shit happens in life and we deal. Can't help those who don't want it. I just go on with my life, knowin' that she changes her mind, she's got my number. She doesn't, then she doesn't."

He's so damn level-headed about this. I admire it deeply. It says a lot about his character, and everything it says, I like. I like a lot, which is probably a bad thing. Nothing about Ryker is supposed to appeal to me. That door was shut, dammit.

"Okay."

We get the stuff at the store in a hurry. Ryker doesn't want to be there any more than I do, so he helps make quick work of it. After unloading and putting away all the groceries, Ryker goes to the bathroom while I go to my bedroom, doing a quick check on my computer and finding nothing.

Coming out into the hallway, a hard chest whose arms come around me tightly runs smack-dab into me. My hands go to his pecs in

113

reaction, palms out. Inhaling, the scent of him and tobacco invade me. Heat thumps through me as my heart picks up speed.

I slowly lift my head. His chin is down, eyes smoldering hot with lust, looking down on me.

The air around us turns static, passing between the two of us. My chest compresses as the world stops and all I can do is take him in. His beautiful face that I've loved for so long. The scruff of his beard, the tattoos on his neck, his dark eyes eating me alive. The entire powerful package that is Ryker right here, in this moment. Nothing else matters. Just him and I.

He dips his head down and finds my lips with his.

I'm lost. My chest plastered against his, squishing my breasts in the most delectable way. Our lips entangled. His hand sifting through my hair. His length growing along my thigh. He tastes so good, and as our tongues collide, the passion escalates. It's like we can't get enough of each other. We can't. I can't.

My brain kicks in, and I yank myself away, shaking my head. "No, we can't do this." I try to back away, but he holds me in place.

Heaving in a breath, he counters, "We can absolutely do this, Austyn."

Pulling out of his hold, the loss of his touch is instant. "You don't understand. If you understood, you'd know." Shaking my head, I dart into my room and lock the door.

He pounds on the outside of it, begging me to let him in. I can't.

Some secrets are meant to be kept.

Some doors are meant to remain closed. Even if they tear you up inside more than you already are.

CHAPTER THIRTEEN

RYKER

She's been in that damn room all day, and every time I ask to come in, she shuts me out. I saw it, though. That spark. She still loves me. Yes, loves me. I've known for many years, but it wasn't the right time. Now is the right time, if she would just let me in. She's locking herself up inside, and it's frustrating as hell.

Head in my hands, elbows resting on my knees, I unseeingly look down at the carpet in front of me, trying to figure out what my next step is going to be with her. What's bothering her is deeper than I thought, and going slow is probably my only saving grace. If I would have rushed it like I wanted and taken what I wanted, she wouldn't have responded. At least I feel better about that decision. Green was right.

Fuck, though, I need to get in there.

The door to the apartment swings open and Emery steps in. "What's wrong?"

I lean back into the couch. "Ya know, death, destruction, famine—

all of it." The joke doesn't come off well, and Emery picks up on it instantly.

She drops her things onto the chair, then sits at the other end of the couch, knee cocked up on it, facing me. "Talk to me."

I think I've done enough talking these past few days with telling Austyn my entire life story. "It's all good. No worries."

"Liar. Austyn turned you down, didn't she?"

Damn woman knows Austyn well.

When I say nothing, she continues. "She's changed. She doesn't want me to see it and tries to cover it up, but she can't, not from me. There's this darkness, like she's almost given up on a lot of things in life. I know what JK did to her was terrible, but she has too much spark, and to watch it fizzle and burn out is killing me."

My chest aches, just as my anger rises.

Emery pats me on the leg. "Know you don't want my advice, but I'm giving it, anyway. She loves you … has for years. I know you're giving her time because of what happened, and that's cool of you and all, but you're going to need to dig harder. She's erected walls around her that need to come down. Get the sledgehammer out."

Her last bit makes me laugh as I lie back on the couch. "Ya know she's gonna be pissed you talked to me, right?"

She shrugs. "If it pulls her out of whatever the hell this is, I don't give a shit. It'll be worth it in the end."

Emery gets up, and I hear the distinct click of her door.

Fuck this.

At Austyn's door, I hear her crying, which tears a deep part of me to shreds. Checking the lock, I go to my truck and get my kit. Within seconds, the door swings open.

Austyn pops up from the bed, tearstains all down her cheeks and eyes red rimmed. "What are you doing?"

I kick the door shut and lock it, tossing all my shit down to the floor. Pulling off my shirt and taking off my boots, she watches me the entire time, her breathing hitching from her crying bout.

Her bed creaks as I climb onto it and grab her body, pulling it to mine and pressing her back to my front.

"Ryker, stop!" she protests, but it's half-heartedly.

I lean into her ear. "Shhh, beautiful. I've got you."

Fresh tears hit her, and her body shakes in my arms.

I fucking hate this shit, but I'm happy I'm here to hold her through it.

It takes a while before her tears dry up and her breathing steadies. I continue to hold her, absorbing it all, taking on her pain and feeling it right along with her. She's too young and beautiful to be feeling any of this.

Suddenly, she turns in my arms, still in my grasp. "Thank you."

I lean in and kiss her forehead. "Anytime." Looking deeply into her eyes, I see her hurt and pain shine through like beacons in the night. Whatever is hurting her is deeper than what happened to her when I found her that day. There's something else lingering that has gouged at her soul, branding it for life.

There's a hurt so deep, so life-consuming that my insides feel it, too.

"Talk to me, baby." I keep my tone calm and soft, not wanting to break this moment, yet wanting so badly for her to confide in me.

She shakes her head as wetness pools inside in her eyes.

"Whatever it is, let me take it on for you."

Austyn continues to shake her head then burrows into my chest, trying to hide from me. I give her that play because she needs it, and because she's wrapped in my arms. Her body begins to shake again, and I hold on tightly.

Kissing the top of her head, I tell her, "You're safe. I got you. No one will touch you again."

Her breaths hiccup, and then she begins to breathe deeply in and out, her tits pressing against my chest.

"I want it to go away." It's so soft I almost don't hear it. "Just make it go away."

Rubbing her back, I ask, "What do you want me to make go away?"

Her breath catches. "The dirt."

"What dirt?"

She clutches my chest. "That covers me."

I tighten my arms around her as it hits me. She feels dirty from what that asshole did to her. She can't get it off her. She can't get clean. That would explain the thirty-minute showers. While I thought she just loved being in the water, Austyn's been trying to scrape him off her. *Fuck.*

Not wanting to scare her, I ask, "What do you want me to do?"

After what feels like hours but is probably only minutes, she lifts her head. "You called me beautiful. Did you mean it?"

"Fuck yes."

She closes her eyes then opens them. "Then make me feel it."

I cup the side of her face, gently moving my thumb back and forth. If she wants me to show her how beautiful she is, how much I desire her, I have no problems doing so. Keeping myself in check is going to be the most difficult part because taking her the way I want isn't an option. She's giving me this, though, and I'll take it.

I graze my nose along hers, hearing her breaths hitch. Then I touch my lips to hers in a sensual kiss. Austyn gives it back to me, but she's hesitant and unsure.

Leisurely, I caress her bottom lip with my tongue, and she opens for me. She loosens up and meets me stroke for stroke, digging her nails into my shoulders.

Cupping the back of her neck, I take it deeper, and then it's as if her brain shuts off. She melts into me, the starchiness in her body completely disappearing as she gives in to it.

She rolls to her back with me hovering over her. I pepper kisses down her neck, moving my hand to the hem of her shirt. As I drag it up, her breathing accelerates, and then it seems as if nerves hit her as she brings her hand to mine, halting my movements.

"Talk to me."

She exhales, almost like she's willing herself to go through this.

"Show me."

She releases my hand.

Looking into her eyes, I feel the go-ahead in them and move my hand up her shirt, feeling her warm skin underneath. Her eyes close, and her hips jolt.

I move the shirt up and up ever so slowly then take it away from her body. She clenches her fists like she wants to wrap her arms around her body and cover herself from me, but she doesn't. This is my cue.

I begin to explore her body with my lips and mouth. Neck, shoulders, chest, abdomen, arms, and fingers. Her small gasps and groans only make me want to do more, so I do.

Reaching around her back, I unlatch her bra. She gives a slight hesitation as I take it off, but then falls back to the mattress.

Giving her nipples special treatment, I lick, nip, suck, and caress her breasts one at a time until her hips are practically bouncing off the bed.

She threads her fingers through my hair, holding me to her chest and pulling my hair in tune with her thrashings on the bed below me.

"Ryker," she gasps, saying words for the first time instead of noises. My cock hardens at hearing my name on her lips while she's like this. It presses painfully against my jeans, but I do my best to ignore it.

I slowly kiss my way down her abdomen to her belly button then her shorts. I pull them and her underwear off gently, which seems to take longer because of her gorgeous long legs. Grazing my hands up those legs, I stare at the wetness between her thighs.

"Ryker?" The uncertainty in her voice has my gaze popping up to hers.

"You're the most beautiful thing in the world. Let me love you."

Austyn's resolve vanishes, a smile playing on her lips that's sexy as hell.

I lean down and kiss her inner thigh, already smelling her, which ratchets up my arousal and desire for this woman.

For me, sex has always been about getting off. This, though, this is so much more. I feel like I'm giving her what she needs. The urge to drive my cock into her isn't as strong as I thought it would be. Just pleasuring her seems to be enough. This has to be a first in my book.

Kissing her, I move to her core, rubbing my nose up her pussy and inhaling her scent, memorizing it. With one large lick, her taste explodes on my tongue. I'm ruined. She is absolutely perfect.

Feasting on her pussy, I can't get enough of her. The more I lick, the more she intoxicates me.

Her hips seem to rotate on their own as she moves her hands to the sheets, gripping them tightly. She's on the brink.

Inserting two fingers, I rub her internal walls that are hot as hell. Austyn's back arches off the bed, a shrill cry coming from her lips as she comes hard. So much so her juices flow out of her body.

Watching her come is now my favorite thing to do. I always knew it would be fantastic, but she went above and beyond my expectations. This is Austyn, though. I should have had no doubts.

She wants me to show her she's beautiful, fine by me.

Attaching my lips to her again, I build her until she explodes a second time.

On the brink of the third, she looks down at me, eyes wild with post-orgasmic lust. "I don't think I can take more."

My lips curve against her. "You sure can, beautiful." I show her again she can take it.

My cock throbs mercilessly, straining to get out and sink deeply into her. The pull to do just that is difficult to shake, but remembering that this isn't about me, that it's about her and showing her how beautiful she is, I will him down, though he's close to coming in my jeans. Fuck, I haven't done that since I was a teenager.

Austyn's body sags with exhaustion, telling me that she's done, at least for now. I spread soft kisses up her body then latch on to her lips where there is zero hesitation this time.

She pulls away, her eyes half-mast. "Thank you."

"Beautiful, any time you want it, you can have it." I kiss her lips once more then pull her head to my chest.

Her breaths even out, and she falls asleep across me. That has to have been the best non-intercourse encounter I've ever had. Hell, it might just be the only one. But fuck me, it was beautiful.

Once I know she's asleep, I ease out from under her, leave the room, and shower. I lather the soap, grip my cock, and remember her taste. It only takes moments before I'm exploding down the drain. The release is empty like many of the others I've had, but I know once I'm inside Austyn, it won't be. Nothing will ever be the same again.

Drying off, I climb back into bed with Austyn, curl her up against me, and fall asleep.

Movement wakes me. Austyn is trying to slip out from under me. I wrap my arms around her waist and pull her back to the bed.

"Morning, beautiful. Where're you runnin' off to?" I kiss her ear.

The tenseness is back in her body, and I hate it.

"To get dressed." She tugs at my arms, but I pull her back flat on the bed and look down at her. Worry lines appear around her eyes, and a hint of panic is inside them.

I kiss her softly on the lips. "I got you, Austyn. Promise you that."

She heaves out a breath. "This can't happen, Ryker. I'm sorry I asked you to do that last night. I shouldn't have."

"That was my pleasure, beautiful. And yes, it will happen … repeatedly." As I move closer, her eyes dilate and her breathing comes quicker, telling me she's turned on just as much as I am.

Her head falls to my shoulder, and her body relaxes. "I just can't, Ryker."

"Tell me why." I keep my tone calm for her, not wanting to scare her away. It's like she's a rabbit. One little noise is going to make her burst out in a run. That isn't an option.

"You don't want to be with me."

Leaning back, I lift her chin with my finger until she makes eye contact with me. "You let me be the judge of that."

She shakes her head. "You don't understand."

"I understand you think you're dirty. That you don't deserve to be happy. Beautiful, I'm here to tell you that shit just isn't true."

She tries to move away, but I hold her steady. "You don't get it."

"I get that I'll spend the rest of my fuckin' life showin' you how beautiful you are every damn day."

She gasps then begins to thrash in my arms. "Let me go!" she screeches, and I do, only for her to jump out of bed and throw on her T-shirt, covering her sexy body. "This can't happen, Ryker. It can't. Not again."

Austyn storms out of the bedroom, shutting the door behind her. I hear the shower turn on and know it's going to be thirty minutes before she comes out. *Fuck.*

My cell rings as I sit on the couch. Austyn still hasn't come out of her room, and it's been over three hours. I look at the ID. *Cooper Calling.*

"Yeah?"

"Clubhouse, now." He disconnects. Fuck, they must have something.

I move to Austyn's door and knock. She doesn't answer. I turn the handle, noting it's locked.

"Austyn, we're going to the clubhouse. Need you out here."

The door swings open moments later, and the shield I've come to recognize is over her. Those walls are back up, strong and secure.

Not giving one fuck, I sweep her in my arms and kiss her hard. After last night, she's not doing this shit. I'll do whatever I have to do to keep them down.

When she relaxes into my kiss, it's then I break away. I grab her hand and pull her out of the place. She must be out of it a bit because she doesn't hesitate.

The clubhouse is hopping with the guys, their ol' ladies, and a bunch of kids.

I lean into Austyn's ear. "Be back. Do not fuckin' leave."

I swear I can hear her rolling her eyes, although that's not possible, as I walk away and into the clubhouse church room where the brothers are sitting around the large table.

"You notice Deke's here. He's family, and that's the end of it," Cruz declares.

This turn of events is a bit shocking, considering prospects normally don't come into the church room, but whatever Cruz says goes.

I lift my chin to Deke, then focus on Cruz.

"How's my girl?" Cruz asks from his spot at the head of the table, his sole focus on me.

Leaning back in my chair, I answer, "Not good, brother."

Silence comes over the room, everyone giving me their attention. Better to get this shit out there now than let it hover.

"Something's goin' on with her that's deeper than what happened with JK. I haven't figured it out yet, but I see it in her eyes."

When Deke rubs his hand over his face, my focus goes to him. "You know somethin'?"

He stares at me, telling me without words that there is, but shakes his head.

"Fuckin' tell me!" I order, slamming my hand down on the table. "I can't help her if I don't know."

"It's not mine to tell."

"We'll discuss this later," Cruz demands, looking at both of us. "You two stay, and we'll deal with this shit. Right now, we have bigger shit that's going to interest you, Ryker." This catches my attention.

"I want JK done, and now."

"Don't we all," I grumble. That fucker needs to pay for putting his hands on Austyn. He needs to hurt for touching what's mine.

Cruz nods at Buzz, who looks at me. "Your girl hacked the computers. She's got all the information we have on JK, and she made all his money evaporate." He gives a soft smile, then on a shrug, says, "She did learn from the best."

My hands go into my hair, giving it a tug as this all computes in my head. All eyes come to me.

"I didn't know shit about it." If I would have, I'd have had her ass.

"Why do you think she'd risk getting caught to get this information?" Cruz asks, though he already knows the answer, just like I do.

"She's going after him. That's why she didn't want a bodyguard. She can't go out and do what she needs to do with me tagging along." And that's why she goes to her bedroom early every night. She's probably on that computer of hers, trying to track him down. *Fucking hell.*

"She's tenacious, but I expect nothing less from my girl." Cruz folds his hands behind his head and leans back. I try to get a read on him, but it's coming up twisted. Part of him is proud of her. Another part is pissed she hacked into the system. And another is seriously concerned.

"What's the score?" I ask, waiting for the bomb to drop.

Cruz looks around, then at me. "You're on her. She doesn't go anywhere, including sneaking out at night, without you knowing about it. Buzz tapped into her computer, so we know what she's doing. I get why she needs to do this, but she will have us at her back. This fucker will go down."

"Right." It's my turn to lean back in my chair. She just earned herself every night with me in her bed, on alert. I don't give a shit what has to be done, no one will touch her again.

"Everyone good with this?" Cruz looks around and gets nods, which surprises the shit out of me. Not even Dagger, who's known for his smart-ass remarks, has anything to say. "Good. Everyone out but Deke and Ryker."

"Dad?" Cooper asks, rising from next to Cruz.

Cruz shakes his head. "Nope. Out."

Cooper reluctantly goes, the door clicking shut behind him.

Deke sits on the opposite side of the table from me with his arms crossed over his chest, obviously not wanting to tell me what the hell is going on with my girl. Yes, *my girl.*

"Brother, you need to tell us what the hell is going on," Cruz says. "This is a club issue now, and we need to know this shit going forward. You don't want everyone to know, fine; that's why I had them leave. But us right here, we need to know."

126

"Can't," he responds without hesitation. "Made a promise before I became part of Ravage. Can't go back on it."

"If I knew something about Riley that was tearing her up from the inside out, that was making her feel dirty and unworthy of any kind of affection, wouldn't you want to know, Deke? Wouldn't you move hell or high water to get the information?"

His jaw ticks slightly. "Yep."

I slam my hand on the table. "Then fuckin' help me!"

"I tell you, she'll never talk to me again. She'll wipe me clean from her."

"And what, her living in pain and cryin' all the time is better than her bein' pissed at you? Seriously, man?" Keeping my anger tapped down is becoming harder and harder. The man can fight. I've seen him in action, but fuck, I want to punch the living hell out of him.

"No, it's not, but this shit isn't easy. I don't go spreadin' people's shit around everywhere."

"Deke," Cruz interrupts. "This is important. We need to know what's eatin' at my little girl. She's not right, and if you can help, we need you to."

"Is this an order?" Deke asks, knowing Cruz can say it and it'll be.

"Do I need to make it one?" Cruz challenges.

Deke contemplates, looking back and forth between us. Coming to a decision, he says, "Bring her in here."

I'm taken aback by his statement, and from the look on Cruz's face, he is too.

"I'm not spillin' her shit. Bring her in here. She'll tell ya if she knows I have to talk," he responds.

"No one comes in here, Deke," Cruz reminds him. This is church.

No one comes in church except patched and prospecting members.

"You want to know, make the exception." Deke doesn't back down from the club president. "Wasn't the man I needed to be for Ravage for a long fuckin' time. Learned shit, lived shit, and fuckin' ate shit. This is not my shit to tell. You bring her in, she knows I didn't break my word, but my hands are tied. She'll do what needs to be done."

Cruz looks at me, and I nod. She'll be pissed, but I'm at the point I don't give a fuck.

"Deke, go get her."

He nods once then leaves the room.

I rub my hands over my face. "This is going to go bad."

"Yep, but we'll have some answers."

"Right." I just hope she'll get through this.

I want to beat the answers out of Deke to spare Austyn any pain. I also want to shake the man's hand for being so bold and standing behind my woman when she felt she had nowhere else to turn. He's an honorable fucking man, even if he pisses me off.

That was my mistake. One that won't happen again. I'll always be the person for Austyn to turn to from now, until my very last fucking breath.

CHAPTER FOURTEEN

Austyn

The soda sits in front of me, untouched, not even popping little bubbles anymore, while conversation flows around me. Here, but not. That seems to be my existence now. Here physically, but mentally distant.

Last night was an idiotic thing to do. To ask him to touch me, to make me feel less dirty. Why did I do that?

Sadness and emptiness creeps inside, knowing he did make it go away. While I was there, in the moment, I didn't feel used, battered, or dirty. He made me feel loved and accepted, like I was beautiful. I let him in and I shouldn't have. Letting him in will only lead to heartbreak.

I can't be what he wants me to be. There's no way. If he ever found out, he wouldn't want me, anyway. He'd know for sure I was damaged and broken.

"Austyn." My name being called tears me out of my thoughts.

I turn around to find Deke standing there with a grim expression on his face.

"Come with me."

Not hesitating, I follow him to the church room.

He looks down at me before opening the door. "You're stronger than you feel," he says strangely then opens the door.

My steps falter. This space is off-limits, has been forever.

"Come in, Austyn," my father calls, and only then do I step into the room.

It has a musty smell to it, like men almost, but there's something else. Pictures line one of the walls, and part of me itches to go look at them. The large wooden table stretches out the length of the room with chairs all around it.

My father holds out the chair next to him. "Have a seat."

I nervously make my way to him. As I sit, Ryker stares at me and Deke stares off into space, looking like he'd love to be anywhere but here.

"Deke," my father says.

By his twisted face, it looks as though Deke's been thrown under the bus.

"Fuck." His focus comes to me, but it's soft and caring. This scares me. This entire thing scares me. My body even trembles.

"What's going on?" I ask with a tremor in my voice, hating it's there, but not being able to control it.

Then the world falls out below my feet, and I fall into a dark hole I can't escape. It's as if I'm Alice, floating toward another world, one where nothing can hurt me and nothing can touch me. Except, it's not. This is reality, and it's horrible.

"They need to know the reason you came to me, Austyn," Deke says.

Time stops. My stomach hits the floor just as the emptiness and void that's inside punches me in the gut. I find myself shaking my head repeatedly, not wanting this to be real, hoping the motion will make it all go away.

Deke lowers his voice. "They want me to tell them the why, but it's yours to tell. I don't want to be in this spot, Austyn, but if you don't tell them, they're going to force their hand so I don't have a choice."

I rise from the chair and find my thumb inside my mouth, chewing on the corners of my nail. My feet find themselves moving back and forth behind my father as everything twists and pulls in my head. I can't tell them. I can't. Just can't.

"No."

"Austyn," Deke calls out, and I stop. "You either tell them, or I have to. I don't want to be the one to do it." His eyes plead with me, telling me he doesn't want to be the one to spread my stuff. I hate this, but I've already asked so much of him. I can't do this to him too. "You're stronger than you think, Austyn."

"Right." I continue my pacing, needing to think on how to approach this and coming up with the conclusion that there is no other way but to rip off the Band-Aid. Deke's had enough pain in his life. I can't add to it, but this pisses me off.

I focus on my father. "Why do you need to know? Why is it your business? If I wanted you to know, I'd tell you. But I haven't, so doesn't that tell you that I want to keep this to myself?"

He rises, coming toward me. "It's eating you up inside. I've told you before that I'm concerned. Deke knows something, and we need to

131

know so we can help you. It's time."

I huff. "Yeah, it's time to tell something I don't want to, and I have to or else Deke will have to violate my trust. This is some fucked-up shit, Dad."

My back is against the wall. I'm out of options.

One look at Ryker and I want to fall into his arms and make it all disappear, but I can't do that, either. I'm pretty sure he started this because of how I was last night, which makes a headache rise.

"Fine, but sit down."

My father raises his brow, but does what I ask. I don't want to look at any of them or see the pity and questions all over their faces. I don't want any of it, yet they've given me no choice. *Fuck*.

The pictures on the wall stare at me. No one says anything, like I shouldn't be looking at them or what have you. My entire focus goes to the pictures. "I went to Grayson because I needed somewhere away from here. Emery talked about Deke living up there, and after some research, I knew it was the spot." I suck in a breath, it doing nothing to fortify my nerves. "I needed to have my pregnancy terminated, and there was a place there. That's why I went to Deke, and that's what he hasn't told anyone."

A chair scrapes along the floor, but I don't turn around to look at who it was. It doesn't matter.

The emptiness in my belly grows, reminding me of the choice I made. The one I have to live with for the rest of my life.

"Baby girl," my father says from behind me, bringing his arms around me and pulling me to his hard body. "Why didn't you talk to someone? Your mother? Me? Someone?"

"And say what? I'm knocked up and I'm not keeping it. Would you have driven me to the clinic?"

"Exactly," my father says, kissing the top of my hair. "You never should've gone through that by yourself."

I exhale loudly. "It's over with now. It's something I live with."

"Can I ask you why you didn't keep it?" This comes from Ryker.

I close my eyes, dreading his question. "No, you can't. And Deke doesn't know, so don't bother asking him. Nor does he know who the father was, so don't ask that question, either. You wanted to know my business, now you do." There is no way in hell they are getting the other part. That isn't happening. This is all they're squeezing out of me. "And I'll remind you, I didn't share willingly. I've given you more than I intended."

This is agony. The walls are closing in, falling on top of me one by one, smashing me into the ground.

"I don't want to talk about this anymore. I want to go home."

"Let's go," Ryker says.

I pull away from my father and go over to Deke, who rises. I wrap my arms around his waist, and he reciprocates.

"I know you didn't want to tell. Thank you for that. But it's out now, so no more."

"So sorry, Austyn," he says, giving me a squeeze.

I look at Ryker. "Not a word. I don't want to talk about it, so don't bring it up."

"Got it," he concedes, surprising me.

After giving a few waves bye, we make our way back to my apartment. I feel raw and cut open, like I'm bleeding everywhere. Not only that … the dirt has come back full force. Not for having to make the choice I did, but for how I became pregnant. For what he did to me.

Life sure loves to play games.

When we enter the apartment, all is quiet. Emery must be out.

Not saying a word, I go to my room, lock the door, kick off my shoes, and crawl into a ball on my bed. Only then do the tears flow.

Moments later, the door unlocks and opens, which I should have known he would do. There's rustling of clothes, and then Ryker is behind me, pulling me against his body.

There is no energy to fight or talk, only to cry and sleep, so that is what I do.

Sleep it all away.

CHAPTER FIFTEEN

RYKER

Fuck me.

Pregnant? She was pregnant, and I had no idea.

As much as I've watched her and kept tabs on her, I never saw it coming. It's like a slap in the face, one that's waking me up to so much more that is Austyn Cruz.

Deke's a good man, keeping that shit tight to him, but we needed to know. The only thing is, I don't have a fucking clue what to do from here. I didn't know what was holding Austyn back, but this isn't what I expected. Not one little bit.

How the hell do I erase this and make it better? *Fuck*.

She says she won't say who the father is, but I'm going to find out. And when I do, he'll wish he never laid a hand on Austyn.

She hasn't brought any guys around the clubhouse in years, and I haven't heard of her dating anyone—that's something I would know. Was it a one-night stand? Even if it was, the fucker needs to be beat down for leaving her to deal with this shit on her own. No man, no real man, would do that.

Yeah, that's going to be my next goal. Find out who this dickhead is and destroy him.

Her breathing evened out a while ago, but no way in hell am I moving. She's mine to protect and care for. I'll do my damnedest to do that.

I wonder if the abortion is why she said she was dirty. She has no reason to feel that way. We all have choices in our life. Regardless, I can see this one is tearing her up.

Asking questions is out, at least for now. She's too raw, and causing her more pain is not my intention.

Austyn's "dirt" isn't on her skin; it's in her soul. The baby, coupled with what JK did to her, she feels like she's unworthy. The pieces are starting to fall into place on why she decided to push me away when I finally got the stick out of my ass.

She doesn't think she deserves me, but she's wrong. I don't deserve her, yet I don't give a fuck. I'll do everything in my power to make sure she feels beautiful, that what has happened in her life doesn't make her filthy in any way. She had no choice with JK. He kidnapped her. That's on him, not her.

I hate that she feels this way. My teeth grind from knowing she's felt this way for months—that's when Deke came home. Even before then, she went to doctor appointments by herself, and then made the decision all by herself. Alone.

That pisses me off. Had I known, I would've been at her back every step of the way, even if she didn't want me there.

Squeezing her a little tighter, I dread tomorrow morning. Austyn will be pissed at me. She's too damn smart for her own good. She'll know I voiced my concerns, and that's why she was brought in.

I'll take the heat for it, let her yell and get pissed at me. Maybe focusing her anger on me will help. Hell, I don't know.

On that note, I close my eyes and drift off to sleep, holding my girl.

"Let go." Austyn's voice comes low and lethal as I wake up from a deep sleep, consciousness not quite there yet.

"What?"

"I said, let go!" she says louder. I can feel the anger pumping off her body. She's pissed and has every right to be. I hate it, but I also respect it.

Releasing her from my grasp, she rolls quickly away from me and off the bed.

"I want you to get out." Her eyes are narrowed into slits, everything directed at me. "Now."

Sitting up, I swipe my hand over my face, knocking the sleep away from them, then rise. Before I go, I say, "This shit doesn't change the way I feel about you. You're beautiful, and I'll stop at nothing to remind you of that."

The door slams behind me, and then Austyn yells some curses loudly and angrily.

One step forward, five steps back with this woman. I knew it, though. *Fuck.*

Entering the dining area, I find Emery is in the kitchen, making something to eat.

"So, I'm guessing she's pissed at ya?" She chuckles. "What'd you do this time?"

I shake my head as I fall into the recliner and lean back.

Emery gets very quiet. That's when I notice Austyn at the mouth of the hallway, fire breathing out of her eyes. Pretty sure, if she could kill me with them, she would.

She storms into the kitchen and opens the fridge, taking out the orange juice then slamming the door so hard the shit on the top shakes. "You might as well know since all of Ravage MC is going to be talking about my business." I make a move to stop her, but her icy glare stops me. "The reason I went up to see your brother was because I had an abortion."

Emery's mouth falls open, her eyes bulging out. "What?" she whispers softly.

"Yep. And asshole over there"—she points at me—"went and told my father that something was up with me, so they were going to force Deke's hand. Therefore, I had to tell."

Austyn reaches into a cabinet, pulling out a glass then pouring some juice into it. Taking a quick drink, she then says, "Yep, so now everyone is going to know my *big* secret."

Emery moves fast, wrapping her arms around Austyn. Whispered words are said that I can't hear. Emery doesn't let go of her for a long time. When she does, they both are misty-eyed. Austyn does everything in her power to avoid me like I'm the plague.

"Do you want something to eat?" Emery asks me, obviously understanding Austyn's cold shoulder.

Just then, a knock comes at the door and I move to answer it. Nox stands on the other side.

"Hello!" he calls out, stepping inside the apartment with a wide smile, and I take this as a sign.

"You stayin' for a while?"

"Yep." He looks over at his sister, still smiling.

"Good. I'm heading out for a bit. Stay until I get back."

Emery gasps from behind me. I know why. I haven't left Austyn's side since I started being her protection. But I know she needs a break from me to gather herself, so I'm going to give it to her. Anyway, I really need to get on my bike and ride for a while.

"Sure, yeah, no problem." Nox's focus skips between the three of us. I don't care what he's thinking.

I make my way to Austyn's room and lace up my boots. Austyn's saying something in the kitchen. I can't make out what it is, but it has a very hostile tone.

Grabbing my keys, I head back into the main room, and yes, Austyn is still firing daggers at me.

"I'm gonna head out for a while. Be back in a bit."

"Good," Austyn says just as I slam the door shut.

I need the wind in my face and sun on my skin. Pulling out a smoke, that's exactly what I do while I think about how I'm going to patch things over with Austyn.

I need a ride. The air, the freedom, and time to soothe the rage inside me that wants to rip JK limb from limb.

This is far from over, my beautiful woman. No, Austyn Cruz, this is just the beginning.

CHAPTER SIXTEEN

Austyn

My bravado leaves once the door closes. I fall onto the couch like a sack of leaves, my energy draining quickly. Closing my eyes does nothing to help the messed-up, twisted feelings swirling inside me, threatening to take over and implode around me. I flex my fingers, hoping to release the tension forming in me, but do a shit job at it.

Being slammed in the face with a two-by-four will do that to a woman. It's exactly what happened to me last night, having to expose something that should've remained buried. It's left me raw and wide open, so wide all the anger is focused on Ryker for starting all this. That's an emotion I hack very well—anger—but it's exhausting.

Nox plops down next to me, patting me on the leg. "What's goin' on with you?"

Staring up at the ceiling, I tell him, "If I'd have known you were coming, I could've saved the big reveal for both of you at the same time."

"Austyn," Emery chastises my smart-ass remark, but I ignore her.

"I went up to Deke's to terminate my pregnancy."

The couch shakes from Nox's response. "Holy fuck."

I don't bother looking at him, but with him being my twin and being together our entire lives, I'm sure his face is turning red and the vein in his neck is starting to thump harder. His fists are probably clamped tight, and I can he's breathing out of his mouth more than his nose.

"Who's the father?" he asks curtly. See? Pissed off.

"That, I'm not discussing. I'm also not discussing why I did it. All you need to know is what I told you." Being a broken record and saying the same things repeatedly is tiring. It must end because my emotions can't keep going through the wringer.

He squeezes my leg, and my focus goes to him.

"Why didn't you come to me?"

"Dad said the same thing. You can get that story from him. I'm tired of talking about it." And I am. I love my family, but bringing all this up is killing me. It's making me relive it. My family can't want that.

"Alright. What the fuck is goin' on with you and Ryker?" He changes the topic instantly to another one that is off-limits. *Lovely.*

"Not talking about that, either, Nox."

Emery falls into the recliner with a cup of yogurt, eating away. "He sleeps with her and lots of noises come from the room."

I grab the throw pillow next to me and toss it at her. Her hand jolts up and yogurt covers her shirt.

"Austyn! What the fuck!" She stands up immediately, going to the kitchen.

"Don't spread my business," I warn. Why does everyone feel the need to do this? It's frustrating.

"I don't get you," Emery says in a huff, dipping a paper towel under the tap then wiping her shirt. "You've wanted him forever. You have him here, in your bed, what you've always wanted, and no-go."

"Did you not hear that he forced my father to make me tell them?"

She tosses the paper towel in the trash. "I get that. It was shit, but before that all came out. Are you punishing yourself because you had an abortion?"

Her question hits me so hard breaths are tough to take. Part of me is. I've known it from the moment I walked out of that clinic feeling empty. Not just that, but add in how the baby was conceived and it's all become a hazy mess in my head. All of it jumbling and twisting into a tight knot that I fear will never be loosened. Instead, it'll eat me alive.

I remember lying on that exam table, everything so sterile and the smell of antiseptic invading my nostrils. The large light shined down from above, then the smaller light at the bottom half of my body. When the doctor asked if I was ready, I wanted to scream and yell, but only responded with a quiet "yes."

Tears fell the entire time. Some for the baby. Some for the life I'd never have. Some for the love I'd never feel. Some for the destruction that had been laid at my feet. All of it compiling into swamp inside my head. A swamp that threatened to pull me down into its depth with each moment that passed by. The water was murky, ready to grab me and pull me under, sucking all the life out of me.

It still feels that way sometimes, when memories of my baby come to me. Like I'm sinking into nothingness, unable to hold on or come up for air.

Ryker knows about the baby, but not the other thing. The other would turn him away from me quickly. It's better this way.

I've grown too close to him lately, allowing him to touch me and comfort me. Those lines need to be formed again, and this time, no going back.

"I guess." My voice is a whisper, not wanting to respond, but knowing a shrug won't cut it for an answer.

She charges over and falls to her knees in front of me, taking my hands in hers. "Whatever your reasons are don't matter, Austyn. It happened and it's over. There is no reason to feel any guilt for it. Decisions are hard, and I suspect this one was the hardest. But there's no guilt. No shame. No self-loathing because of it. I'm not saying go skip off into the sunset and never think about it—it's part of your history. But hurting yourself for it isn't an option anymore, Austyn. You deserve to be happy and loved."

Tears well up and roll down my cheeks. I needed those words from her. God, how I've needed them. Being alone through it, I'd often wonder if I made the right decision or if I ever deserve to have a baby again in my life because of what I did. Let alone to ever be happy. Why should I be happy when my baby isn't here? It doesn't seem right.

Emery's words, though … they're what I needed to hear because the guilt is eating me alive. If they knew the reason, they would understand, but they won't know. Emery is right; it doesn't matter the why because it's over. At least that part of it. The darkness inside me is still seeking vengeance, though, but it happened and now I need to move on.

"Thank you," I choke out, and as I do, a weight lifts from my shoulders. One that's been holding me down for months and months.

The tightness in my chest begins to loosen, and I can breathe a bit more than before.

"You're not going to like what I'm going to say next."

I toss my head back to the couch. I just had an epiphany in my life and now she's throwing me a curveball.

She taps me on the leg, and I lift my head.

"I know you're pissed at Ryker."

"Emery …" I warn, but she doesn't stop, just railroads right over me.

"He did you a favor." My body jolts as heat sprouts in all directions. "Hear me out." I give a slight nod, barely containing myself. "I'm not saying he should be sharing your shit, but you've grown up in this club, and you know how things are. It came from a good place. I know it. Ryker loves you, Austyn."

Oxygen will not fill my lungs, and my heart stops. Everything I've always wanted comes at the worst time possible. As is my luck, it seems.

"He does," Emery continues when words don't come for me. "He caters to you here. I've watched it. *You need a pillow, beautiful?* Or, *You can cook for me every night,* as he shovels in your food like he's a starving man. Anywhere you want to go, he's there, and it's not because he was told to do so. It's because he wants to be here, Austyn."

Sucking in much-needed air, my brain tries to compute everything she's telling me, but it feels like a hamster on a wheel, running around and around.

"He did you a favor by pushing that information out of you. Now your family knows, and you don't have to hide it. You don't have to feel that pressure alone. You have us to lean on. You want to be pissed at him now, so be it, but he did it from a good place, not being evil and

145

vindictive."

"Yeah, what she said," Nox throws in, in typical Nox fashion, and a chuckle escapes me.

It feels good to have someone to talk to about this, there's no denying Emery that one.

I sag further into the sofa, not knowing what to do. Be pissed, not be pissed. It sure does take a lot out of a person—being angry, keeping it up all the time.

My life is a tangle of webs that need to be untangled and let loose.

He's been gone for four hours. Nox has called him three times, wanting to leave, but can't, because of me. I told him to go, that we'd be fine, but he gave me the evil stare in return. As the time ticks on, my stomach begins revolting, tying itself into knots.

"Would you stop pacing and biting that damn thumb," Nox says gruffly, looking at his phone like it'll magically ring any second.

Ripping my thumb away from my teeth, not realizing it was there in the first place, unease washes over me. Is he coming back? Is he hurt? Is he so pissed off at me he can't be in my presence?

Time moves slowly, like the tick of the clock has taken way too much valium.

Five hours, and no Ryker. Butterflies swarm in my stomach.

Six hours, and no Ryker. My mouth dries. Drinking water doesn't help.

Seven hours. Pacing the floor.

When the rumble of a bike can be heard, I dart to the window just as Ryker kills the bike and pulls off his helmet, shaking his head so the hair lands in a sexy way. He makes quick work of entering the apartment, and my feet lead me right to him. I throw my arms around his neck, letting the worry and anxiety fall away and enjoying the feel of him in my arms, safe and in one piece.

"Hey," he says.

I don't move. Instead, I squeeze him harder, and he kisses the top of my head. We stand there for long moments until I finally get myself under control and step back.

"I'm happy you're here, but I'm still pissed at you," I tell him then turn away, heading to the couch and falling without any grace.

"What the fuck, man?" Nox says, already moving toward the door. He loves me, but his life is busy and something he can keep to himself. "Been fuckin' callin' you for hours."

Ryker pulls out his phone. "Yep, I see you have. Been ridin'; didn't hear."

"Next time, we're setting a time limit." Nox calls out his byes and is gone, slamming the door behind him.

Ryker sits next to me on the couch, leaving room between us. The space feels like a thousand-mile deep void, so close yet so far away.

He exhales. "When I was asked how you were, I answered honestly. That I'm worried about you, that you have something inside that is eating at you, and I need to help you—whatever it is—because I want to see the smiles and laughter again. That's when your father called it. But, beautiful, I wanted Deke to talk, too, so I'm not puttin' it all on your dad. Deke went to bat for you. That man is loyal to the core."

I repeatedly twist my hands in my lap, listening to him, unsure of how to feel. I want to be pissed and smack him upside the head. Part of me wants to storm out of the room or yell at him, but none of that comes. The pain is there, though, like he sliced through my heart and soul, leaving me bleeding in front of everyone, exposing me for the horrible person I am.

"I'm sorry, Austyn." He turns his body fully toward me, cocking his knee up and pressing it into the back of the couch. "Would you have told me if I asked?"

"No." The answer is immediate. I would've gone to the grave with it, which had been the plan all along. No one would ever know. It's another reason JK needs to be dealt with. He can never reveal it.

It was going to be the one secret that would never come to light, but that was all a lie, which scares me.

"How do you feel now that it's out there?"

I cross my arms over my chest, trying to cover the hole I feel there. I need a shield of protection and a way to guard myself. Two of them, because I feel very exposed, like he's cutting me open raw, stripping me down to nothing.

My skin prickles with awareness, and a shiver races down my spine. Hesitation creeps in, coating me in a shroud. If only I could disappear under it.

Taking a deep breath, I answer, "Scared about what everyone will think of me. That they'll look at me differently." I look down at my hands, not wanting to make eye contact with him. "Relieved that I don't have to hold it all in anymore. But I'm still pissed at you."

His smile is wide and one I could get lost in, unable to break away from. Whenever he's around, the keeping my distance thing lasts a minute before the walls just crumble. I should be pissed at him for that, too; add it to the shit pile.

"Be pissed, beautiful. That's fine. I'll take it. But you don't need to be scared. Who gives a fuck what others think? That has no bearing on you whatsoever. Their thoughts and opinions are theirs, not yours. Whatever they say or how they act is on them, not you. Not only that, I'll beat the shit out of 'em."

My lips tip up as his words wrap around me like a warm blanket. A blanket that is covering the bloody wounds deep inside, slowly stopping the flow.

We sit in silence, but it's comfortable. The anger is still there, but it's fizzled quite a bit. I'm not sure what to make of that.

A yawn escapes me, and before I can say anything, Ryker has my head on his chest, remote in his hand, and I'm fast asleep.

The night ended up chaotic. My mother, father, Angel, GT, and pretty much anyone in the clubhouse they could round up, came to my small apartment. They spilled out the front door and balcony, each of them with pointed stares at me. They already knew, so I was happy I didn't have to tell the story again.

They were there for moral support, which felt nice. My mother, on the other hand, was pissed.

"Austyn! I can't believe you didn't tell me this," my mother says, closing the door to my room for privacy. She'd been waiting to attack and found an opening.

"Mom ..."

"Don't you mom me. I would've been there for you. We could've talked, and I could've helped you. You didn't have to do this alone."

I see the instant my mother's anger turns to sadness as her face drops.

"It's over with now. Thank you for that. I need it, but it's over, and there's no reason now to be upset about it."

That was the moment she wrapped me in her arms and hugged me so tightly I thought she would break me.

The other kicker was the appearance of Leah, which is still rolling around in my head.

"Austyn," Bristyl introduces. "This is Leah, Green's woman."

Giving a soft wave, I say, "Hi."

My legs tremble, knowing exactly what this woman has gone through and noting its similarities to my situation.

Leah is beautiful with short dark hair and brown eyes.

"Thought we could go in your room and chat," Bristyl announces before leading us to my room. I've already been in here once with my mother. Maybe this should be the party stop, instead.

Leah fiddles with her hands, worry lining her face. Her chest heaves up and down rapidly.

Bristyl puts her arm around Leah, and she jumps, then she seems to be okay.

"You don't have to talk about anything," I reassure her, seeing a small bit of relief cross her features.

I watch as she breathes in and out slowly. It's an amazing thing to watch, when a woman pulls up courage from down deep.

"It does get better," she starts, having my full attention. "It's hard. There's pain, and the fear will sometimes override you, but you need to ride it out. It's not easy. It actually sucks, but it's necessary. It's been months and months since ..." *She shakes her head. "And I still have a hard time talking about it. But each day is better. Keep your chin up and never let the past define who you are. Never let what happened to you take away your happiness in life, because you only get one. One life*

to make work for you and do the best you can. Don't let the actions of someone else dictate how that life will be lived."

She exhales deeply and sits on my bed, looking as if she spent every last bit of energy she had inside her to say those words. I hate that she's so broken. Is that what I look like?

"Thank you, Leah." I sit next to her. "It is hard, and I appreciate you saying those words."

She looks up at me, her eyes haunted.

"Seems you need to follow your own advice." I give her a soft smile in hopes she'll be able to relax a bit.

"I'm working on it. Every day is a challenge, but it's coming."

After that conversation, fatigue from everything settled deeply inside my bones.

Ryker ended up sleeping on the couch. I told him I needed space, which wasn't a lie. I used that time to try to build my walls back up and use concrete to keep them in place. It didn't work. Leah's words continually ran through my head like alarm bells, not shutting off throughout the night.

This morning when Ryker drove me to work, he grabbed my hand and kissed the top of it, saying nothing, but his touch was everything. Comforting and honest.

Now he sits in the salon's waiting area, playing on his phone, moving his thumbs quickly across the screen.

Two women, a couple of chairs down, ogle him, their eyes filled with lust and want. Not that they can be blamed for that. Ryker is hot; there's no question about that.

Life must go on, and there is work to be done.

My mom always said that the true measure of a woman is how they deal with problems. Now that task lays directly in my lap.

"There you go, Althea. All curled and colored." I turn her so she faces the mirror, and her face lights up.

Her hand goes up to her hair. "Oh, I love it! Thank you, dear!"

That is the one thing all clients do. As soon as I get their hair done, they have to run their hands through it like they have some magical touch that will make the hair just perfect. To each their own. You get used to it.

Althea hands me a tip then moves to the front of the building to the cashier counter. After cleaning up, I walk up to Ryker, purse in hand, and his head comes up from the phone.

"Time to go."

He moves quickly. So quickly I try to hold in a laugh. He doesn't like it here, and I can't blame him one bit. Being around women all day is hard, and I'm one who he doesn't get a break from.

Sometimes women are catty or talk behind each other's back. They'll make plans with two of them and leave a third out. Women, at least here at the salon, are so different than men.

Men, they'll fight it out and be down with whatever is bothering them. Women can hold a mean grudge. Something that happened years ago, they can hold it over your head forever. My mother, though, is a fighter. Put up or shut up. I go with her way of thinking.

"Let's go to dinner."

My stomach takes that moment to rumble. That's the thing about Ryker—it doesn't embarrass me one bit.

"Dinner it is."

Nerves light off like firecrackers as we sit in a booth at the local mom and pop shop. Him on one side, me on the other.

There are so many things to talk about, yet I don't want to talk about any of them. I wish I could just disappear sometimes and not be an adult. Forget having to make decisions and thinking. Just be free again to think the world is perfect and the bad stuff will never touch me.

That'll never happen again. Adulting sucks.

After we order, the waitress brings us our drinks. I twirl my straw in my cup, knocking the ice around, not sure what to say or what to do at this point.

Ryker breaks the silence. "Talk to me, Austyn. I know you're pissed at me, but talk to me."

I'm not even sure what to say, so I just open my mouth and let it roll. "Never again, Ryker. Swear to me that as long as we know each other, you will never ever repeat my business to others."

He leans back in his seat. "I reserve the right to break the rule if it means helping you."

"No. That's not going to work."

He leans into the table, his elbows on it, his face close to mine. "It has to work because I'll do whatever I have to, to keep you safe. I'll break anyone who stands in my way of it. You will be safe, and you will be loved. There's no question about that in my eyes."

While what he said was sweet, it also pisses me off.

I clasp my hands in front of me, lacing my fingers together so I don't scratch his eyeballs out. "So, you'll tell the club everything I tell you?"

"You're not listening. I said I'll do whatever I have to, to protect you. If that means pushing something like the other night, then so be it. It doesn't mean I'll go to the club, or anyone for that matter, and talk about private things. There's a huge fuckin' difference there."

"How am I supposed to trust you, Ryker?" That's the biggest thing right now, and it kills that I don't. Before, I trusted him enough to touch me and make me come several times. I've trusted no other man to do that ever. I gave him that part of me, which is really the only thing I have to give—me.

Ryker loves you, Austyn. Emery's words ring in my head, making my heart crack. This is why I need to stay away from this man. I knew the friend thing wouldn't work. My feelings for him are too strong, and having him around me all the time only reinforces them. It's too difficult to keep them at bay.

Part of me wants to tell him why I had to get rid of my baby. That way, he'll know and won't want anything to do with me. I'll be done with all this. I can focus on JK without Ryker clouding up my thoughts all the time, knowing he'll disappear without a glance back.

"I'm going to ask Dad to assign me a new bodyguard."

Ryker's jaw drops, and it takes him a moment to respond. "No fuckin' way. I fucked up, but you're not gonna push me away. You're not dirty. You're fuckin' beautiful, and I'll make sure you know it."

I shake my head. "This is too hard for me." The words escape before I want them to.

"Being around me is too hard? Why is that, Austyn? Because you have feelings for me and you're fighting them?"

"No." The denial is immediate.

His voice dips low, almost threatening. "Don't lie to me, Austyn."

"Don't you get this? It can never work between you and me."

"It has been for the last few weeks," he counters without hesitation.

He has me there. Despite the hiccup the other night, things have been going well. Too well.

"I can't just wipe it away and pretend the other night didn't happen."

"Stop deflecting."

I stomp my foot in frustration right as the waitress brings our food out, placing our plates in front of each of us, then leaves.

"Can we just eat and talk about this again ... never?"

"When we get home." He takes a bite of his burger.

This discussion is going to rip me apart.

Can't he see my resolve is broken? Can't he feel the pain this causes me?

I study Ryker. His eyes meet mine. Confusion laces with my determination.

He wants to help me.

Emery once again plays in my mind. *Ryker loves you.*

The more I try to untangle myself, the deeper I seem to pull myself in.

CHAPTER SEVENTEEN

RYKER

Screaming tears from Austyn's room in a murderous cry. I jump up from the couch, gun in hand, and charge down the hallway. Her door is locked, so I kick it open. The wood goes flying, smashing into the wall behind it just as Austyn pops up from bed, fear and worry on every bit of her face. Her breathing is hard and ragged. Sweat glistens off her, making her hair stick to her body.

Glancing around the room, I find everything is secure.

I rush to her, sitting on the bed. "What's wrong?"

Her eyes are glazed over. She's here, but she's not.

"Austyn!" Her name said loudly snaps her into the present, the fog evaporating. She looks at me panicked, but it's not from me; it's from her dream. It has ahold of her still.

I pull her stiff body into my arms, wrapping her in my warmth. She doesn't do anything except breathe, her body stiff. She's remembering, and I hate that I can't wipe those memories away and take on her pain.

Rubbing her arms up and down, she begins to get her breathing regulated. I maneuver us so my back is to the headboard and her body is against my bare chest.

"You're alright, beautiful. I got you."

She nods absently.

We sit there for a while, me rubbing her back in even strokes and her coming out of wherever her mind had taken her. Not wherever. I know where it took her. I hate that I can't go inside her head and erase those memories for her.

Her head comes up and she sits up on the bed next to me, her head in her hands. "Sorry," she whispers.

"I've slept in this bed numerous times, and you didn't have any nightmares."

Her vacant eyes rip my soul in half, but her words gut me deeper than a blade ever could. "That's because you were with me."

That's enough of this.

I lie fully down on the bed and pull her to my chest. She doesn't fight, just relaxes against me.

"Sleep, beautiful. I got you."

She finds sleep, but I have a difficult time.

Damn woman is driving me crazy. I've given her two days. That's all she's getting. I'm not sleeping on the fucking couch one more night. Being patient and gentle is only getting me so far. She needs to get over this hump she's trying desperately to put between us. Tonight is the last straw. No more sleeping alone for her.

The wall she's wanted to put in place isn't working. As much as Austyn wants it to, it's not. When she doesn't think, she leans into me or touches me like it's the most familiar thing she's ever done in her life.

Those are the times, the unguarded, that tell me how she really feels. Those are the ones I'm listening to now.

She can fight it all she wants, but she's not going to win this battle. Her brain just needs to catch up with her body and heart so we can be on the same page.

This is a long shot, but I've been to the gym with Austyn and seen she can kick some serious ass, so this should be a walk in the park for her.

"Come on; put some tennis shoes on and let's go."

She looks up from the magazine she's been staring at aimlessly. "Where are we going?"

"Surprise. Let's go."

Her hand goes to her hip in that sexy stance that she thinks intimidates me. "I don't like surprises." This is so untrue. The past three years for her birthday, her mother has given her little things from out of left field that she never would've thought of. One was a locket that used to be Ma's, then Princess', and now Austyn has it. She loved it so much she cried.

"Bullshit."

"Don't you bullshit me," she snaps back.

I enjoy her spark coming through, even if she's a little irritated with me. It makes it all the sexier.

"Call it like I see it. Time's a wastin'. Get a move on, woman."

Those damn block walls she still tries to put up around her every day are what I fight every moment. She hides behind them so damn often and won't allow herself to be happy. She needs to come to terms with her abortion and what happened with JK. It's a shit hand, but she needs happiness.

Austyn huffs out a hasty breath, but does what I asked and goes into her room, coming out with her lips in a flat line. Goal for the day: make her smile as much as possible.

I open the door. "After you, beautiful."

She says not a word, but moves out the door. Securing it, we walk to the parking lot.

"Are we going on your bike?" Her face lights up, and the tension in her body seems to relax.

"Absolutely." I lean in close to her ear and whisper, "And you have to hold on tight."

Her body jolts, and I swear I hear her sigh. Yeah, still fighting it.

Sledgehammer is out and ready for business. She better watch the fuck out.

When I grab her hand to lead her to the bike, she doesn't recoil.

I love my ride, a Harley Davidson Night Rod. Everything is straight black with chrome tips on the exhaust. The design of the bike is all curves. It's a fluid piece with no fucking sissy bar.

Swinging my leg over, I motion for her to get on the bitch seat. With a smirk that I'm counting on as a smile, she throws her leg over and straddles my beast beautifully.

Always knew she'd look gorgeous on the back of my bike.

When she brings her hands to my hips, a chuckle escapes me. "That's not gonna work, beautiful." Grabbing her hands, I pull her arms around my body tightly, her front pressed to my back, exactly how it should be.

"Shit!" she says, moving her arms, but I grab them. "I have to braid my hair really quick." I let go as she does her thing. When she wraps herself around me again, I know she's ready to roll. I hand her the helmet, which she puts on without arguing, and then pulls out her sunglasses.

We take off through the streets of Sumner, then hit the open road.

When I got my first bike, I fell in love and have had one ever since. It was freedom from the confines of my life. I was so lost and broken from my family's rejection of me that I needed something to loosen their hold. No, I didn't like their way of life, but to be literally kicked out from the only family you've known, it rides on your shoulders for a long time. Not saying that I'm not happy it happened, but it was a rough time in my life. My bike is my escape. Ride free, baby.

With the rumble of my bike between my legs and Austyn wrapped around my body, there isn't a single place on this fucking planet I'd rather be than here in this moment. I've had girls on the back of my bike before, but never someone I truly loved and cared about. This right here makes me feel whole in a way I never thought I'd find.

Love.

Yes, I love this woman.

There's no stopping because the destination can wait. It's the ride that matters now.

She leans with me through the curves, and it's sexy as hell. Love that my woman knows how to ride a bike. Not that I had any doubt; she did grow up around them.

Austyn's entire body relaxes into me, her head briefly tilting to the side, and her arms get tighter. Yeah, she's feeling this, just like I am. *No running, little mouse.*

We ride until the tank gets low, and then fill up before continuing. Hours in the sun and wind with a beautiful woman is the best day imaginable.

We don't have to talk. The way she molds to me, the way the gravel passes under us as we are one unit. says it all.

I squeeze her thigh as I turn off, letting her know of the change in plan. Then I pull the bike to a stop and cut the engine. Austyn climbs off the back, her legs a little unsteady.

"Sorry. It's been a long time." The smile she gives me is breathtakingly sexy. It steals my breath.

Holding her up until she gets her sea legs straight, I join her on the ground as she looks around at where we are. "What are we doing here?"

The building is an old warehouse about an hour outside of Sumner. I only found it by googling it, so it better fucking be what it's supposed to be.

"This is the surprise."

"And here I thought the ride kicked ass," she teases, surprising the shit out of me. I don't let that show. Instead, I give a sexy smile, enjoying her relaxed state and the Austyn I've missed for a long damn time.

"It did. Come on." Grabbing her hand, we walk into the building where sounds of whistles and shoes hitting pavement echo throughout. When I thought about what to do, this was the first thing that came to mind. It also has another purpose, which I'm hoping she finds.

Austyn looks around, her eyes widening. "I've always wanted to do this."

I lean in close. "I know."

Her cheeks turn a rose color as she glances away from me shyly. I don't let it go, though.

Moving in front of her, our eyes connect. "Told you I've paid attention all these years, beautiful. I'm not shittin' ya." I bend down and put a peck on her lips, and she gasps.

Not wanting to ruin what we have so far in this trip, I pull us toward the check-in, and then we get suited up.

The instructor is a man. A man who's looking at Austyn's ass. Not liking that one bit, I get in his face.

"You keep your eyes on her face or me, and you have no problems."

His boyish face turns pale. We understand each other. Good.

"Alright!" He claps his hand energetically, recovering quickly from my threat. "Have you ever been rock climbing before?"

"Nope. It's my first time," Austyn tells him on a smile.

Score another for me. The instructor keeps his eyes where they need to be. At least I don't have to beat the shit out of him and ruin the day.

"Nope."

"Good. Your harness is going to keep you from falling." He shows us how the ropes connect to the lines above and how they all work together to keep us safe. "Now that doesn't mean for you to rely on them, because you want to make it up the wall and ring that bell up there." He points up high, showing us there is indeed a bell at the top of wall.

"Always think about where you're going and how you're going to get there. Not only will you use your entire body, you will use your brain too."

Austyn jabs me in the stomach with her elbow.

"What?"

She leans in close just so I can hear. "Your brain, not your dick."

My cock instantly jumps to attention. She's never been blatantly forward with me. This is a huge step. I'll take it.

"It's already thinkin' of you, beautiful."

Those cheeks blaze.

"So, are you ready?" the instructor asks, breaking our moment. *Fucker.*

"Sure thing!" Austyn says, excitement bubbling off her. Yeah, this was a good idea.

The instructor moves the wall and demonstrates where to put our legs and arms. "Make sure you have a tight grip with one hand, always. Your foot could slip at any time, so you need to be prepared."

I stretch out my muscles, moving my arms back and forth to loosen them up. Normally, I use the clubhouse gym to let off steam, but it's been a while. Even going to the gym with Austyn, I didn't push myself too hard. This, I have a feeling, is going to be a test.

"You're all set." He claps again, and I guess it's the sign to start because Austyn attacks the wall, not looking over at me once. It's mesmerizing, but I get my ass in gear.

In my peripheral vision, I watch as she grasps each of the pegs, maneuvering her feet to correspond with her hands. Her brows are knit in concentration as she eats up the distance between the floor and the top.

Focusing on my task, I make my way up the wall, thanking my arm strength. This is definitely a workout.

"Shit!" Austyn growls, falling from the wall.

I reach out just at the ropes grasp her and breathe out a sigh of relief she's safe. Not giving two shits about making it to the top, I release myself and fall to the floor with her.

She's breathing in and out heavily, looking at the wall like it's the enemy and she needs to conquer it.

Inside, I sigh. This was my entire point of bringing her here. Her nightmares invade her, taking her over and crushing her. I want her to come to terms that she can beat it back. She has the strength to fight it away. To get her determination back and conquer her life.

Austyn is so much stronger than she thinks she is.

"You okay?"

"This wall is mine," she growls.

I don't hide my amusement.

"What are you laughing at?"

"Not a thing. Show me what ya got."

Her brow lifts questioningly, but she says nothing as she attacks the wall again.

I follow. My second attempt, I don't fall back to the floor with her when she trips up her feet. Instead, I go all the way up to the top and hit the bell. When the rope brings me back down, she has her hands on her hips, eyeing the wall again, seeming to make some sort of strategy.

Pulling her in for a kiss right now wouldn't be the ideal thing, considering she wants to conquer this and I want her to do so, as well.

Moving up behind her, I brush my body against hers. "Think. Be patient. And tear it up."

Austyn nods and goes at the wall.

Standing back, watching her, I can see her vibrating with determination. When I see her second-guessing herself, I yell up, "Don't. You got this."

She actually nods, acknowledging me, before she goes back at it.

She continues up the wall, and not until she rings the bell do I let out the breath I was holding.

When she floats back down to the floor, I wrap her tightly in my arms. Her beautiful smile is wide, and as much as that's my goal for the day, I need her lips, so I take them.

Our hot bodies collide, her hands coming to the side of my face as I deepen the kiss. She tastes so damn good that I don't want to stop. She pulls away first, eyes half-mast and so damn sexy.

"I did it," she whispers.

"Fuck yeah!"

Austyn laughs hard in my arms, a sound I'll never get tired of hearing.

"Let's race!" Her energy pulses off her, and I suck in this moment like a starving man.

"And what do I get if I win?" The low rumble in my voice catches her attention.

She focuses on my mouth. "A kiss."

"Like the one I just got?"

She nods with a glint of promise in her eyes. I'll take it.

"And if you win?"

"Um … A kiss?"

I toss my head back and laugh hard and deeply. "So, either way, I'm gettin' a kiss from you?"

Shyly, she says, "Yeah."

"How 'bout a back massage?" I suggest. Any way to get my hands on her, the better. The thought of rubbing my hands down her body has my blood all going south.

Her pupils dilate, telling me she likes the idea. I do too. I do too.

"Okay."

Squeezing her hip, I tell her, "I'm winnin' this."

"You'd rather rub me down than kiss me?" she accuses playfully.

I sweep a tendril of hair out of her face. "That rub down will hopefully end in a kiss."

"Alright, let's do this!" the instructor says.

I seriously want to punch him. Instead, I glare.

Breaking apart, we stand in front of the wall, and I strategize, plotting the steps and moves I'm going to make.

"I'm winnin' this," I tease.

"Oh, no. This is mine," she challenges back, and I will my cock to stand down. No way I'm going to win this with a raging hard-on.

"Ready!" the instructor yells. "Go!"

I push my body hard and fast. She's gaining on me, nipping at my waist. My height is an advantage, and I use it fully.

"Ryker!" she calls, my focus slipping as she smiles and reaches about a head above me. *Shit!*

"Not playin' fair. I like it."

She laughs as I gain on her. We're neck in neck.

At the last moment, I pull ahead, reaching for the bell and slapping it hard.

"Ahhh!" she screams, hitting it next, only a few seconds after me. She glares. "Dammit!"

My laugh is deep and rumbles through my body like a vibration. "All's fair in love and war." Without another word, I push off the wall and fall back down to the ground, Austyn following behind me.

"You know it's all because of your height." This woman is fucking hilarious as she comes up with the reasons she lost. A little competition never hurt anyone, and she proved to herself that she could do it.

"Did you climb the wall?"

"Yes," she snaps. From all the years watching her, I know she's not mad, just frustrated with herself for not pushing a little bit harder.

"Did you do it the first time?"

"No."

Stepping closer, I slide my hands up her arms. "The second you didn't, either. Then you did it. Then you raced me up to the top and made me work for it. You. You're stronger than you think, Austyn. You're the strongest woman I know."

She softens, her body swaying toward me. Taking full advantage, I grab the back of her neck and pull her to me in a searing kiss. She gives, and I take. I give, and she takes in a dance that makes the air around us electrify.

A cough comes, and Austyn pulls away. I glare again at the motherfucking instructor. He pales.

"My next group is here."

"Good, because we're leaving."

Austyn chuckles as we get out of our contraptions, obviously feeling my tension and the need to pound something.

We leave in a rush through the doors and out to my bike, our hands clasped together. Pulling her around to my front, I land my lips on hers once more. This time, she's more hesitant, but gives in. Her lips are so damn soft.

When we break, it isn't because of some asshole; it's because we can't breathe and need oxygen.

"Guess I got my kiss," she jokes.

"Many more where that came from."

Her eyes close, and pain laces through them when she opens them again. She's putting the walls back up. Not willing to let her, I kiss her again. I don't give her a moment to think after. Instead, I pull her to the bike, and then we take off like a shot, her arms around my waist, holding on tight. This is where she needs to be.

When I get her home, I'll show her exactly how good we are together.

CHAPTER EIGHTEEN

Austyn

My heart races as the bike speeds down the road. Holding on to Ryker is amazing and more than I ever dreamed it could be. His body is so hard, and I can feel each of his muscles when I flex my fingers. I swear I feel him shiver, but it must just be the bike.

This is all my fantasies wrapped in a sexy package, and when he kissed me, it was the cherry on top of the sundae. His lips are magnificent. Not that I have much experience with lips or kissing, for that matter, but his are perfect.

There's so much in a kiss. The connection between two people, allowing the passion to take over, even just for a moment. Letting the feelings you want to say express themselves through a kiss when you know you can't. I poured my heart into each of them earlier, not letting the past interfere.

Now, as we pull up to the apartment, it's like we're back in the real world and everything before lays shattered at my feet.

I'm still the girl with dirt and grime covering my body inside and out, with secrets she doesn't want anyone to know. I'm still the girl who wants revenge on the man who made me this way. I'm still the girl who's loved the man I'm holding on to for so long that it physically hurts that I can't have him.

Maybe I can pretend that everything is great for a while. That my life isn't a big pile of shit on a cracker. That I was never touched or had to terminate my pregnancy. That I was never captured the second time and made to bleed. If I could pretend all those things didn't happen, then maybe I can give this a shot with him.

A hollow feeling comes over me like a black veil of misery. All that is just stupid. There is no pretending a life I want. It will just be too hard to survive once it all falls at my feet, because it will. The dirt on me will make it so.

The only man who knows of the true dirt that's on me is JK. If he would come out of his rabbit hole so I could find him, then maybe, maybe once he's gone and the threat of anyone knowing my past has evaporated, I could have the life I crave. Or maybe those are just dreams I don't deserve to have.

If I could eliminate him, destroy him, he wouldn't be able to tell my past. I hate being such a conflicted, fucked-up mess.

When the bike stops, I climb off, getting my legs in order quickly. Ryker follows as I start to make my way back into the apartment. Before I can get there, though, he pulls me to him, our bodies so close I feel him everywhere.

"Just for tonight, it's all gone. There's nothing but you and me in this world. There are no pasts. There are no expectations. There is only this—what we feel for one another. All the other bullshit is gone, vanished. Only we exist."

My heart thumps so hard I'm sure he can feel it against his chest, pumping away. This sounds magnificent. Perfect. To just forget about everything. To live in the moment. Live in the now with Ryker. To experience something with him that I never have before. I'd be lying to myself if I didn't think it was going to end up in bed together if we gave in.

Can I hack that? Leave the feelings aside after the daylight comes again? Go on about our lives like the night never happened?

No, I can't. It will hurt. It will kill. But it will be everything. Something I may never get again in my life.

It's stupid and careless. Reckless and destined to hurt me more than I already am.

My heart and head battle it out.

Ryker's lips come to mine. This kiss penetrates the walls, shining light into the hole my heart has felt since everything came down on me. It fills the empty and shines bright. I want this. I need this. I need him to show me it's not painful and it doesn't have to shred my insides. Just for one night.

He penetrates my stare, and I get lost in his brown depths as they suck me in. He's giving me everything I've ever wanted.

"Yes."

Ryker's smile turns his serious face into one that makes women swoon, including me.

He pulls my hand, leading me into the apartment. "I'll order delivery. We'll eat, and I owe you a back rub."

Panic slams me hard. This is going to hurt.

We eat in front of the television like we've done so many times before, but this time there is a thick tension in the air that's hanging over us like a cloud. Nerves rattle me from every part of my body, from the tips of my fingers to my toes.

A woman my age shouldn't fear sex. She should enjoy it. Relish in it. Unfortunately, my introduction to it was horrible. What if I'm bad in bed? What if I don't do things right? I've watched porn, don't get me wrong, but that's nothing on doing it for real. Because, who am I kidding? If it's just Ryker and me, there will be touching. There will be sex. I've felt his hard erection on my back, waking up to it more times than I can count. He wants it, and deep inside, I do too.

Ryker takes my plate from me then heads to the kitchen. When he comes back, I'm a big ball of nerves, like I'm sixteen again, trying to get this man's attention. Now I have it, fully, and I'm scared.

He sits next to me, while I twist my hands as the heat from anxiety rushes through me.

"Maybe we shouldn't do this."

Ryker reaches over and pulls me to him, negating the gap we kept while we ate, and wraps his arm around me. "Just relax, Austyn."

Easy for him to say. He's done this …

I stop myself from those thoughts. I don't want to know that.

As we watch television, my body relaxes into him. He repositions us then begins to massage my feet. It feels so damn good, losing me in the sensations. The kneading and rubbing gets kinks out I didn't know were there.

"Lie on your stomach."

I do as he says. His hands begin to do magical things. The strength in them is amazing, but it's the tenderness that warms my heart.

174

Forgetting about the television, I close my eyes and enjoy the feel of his hands on me.

My shoulder.

My upper back.

My lower back.

My legs.

My arms.

Every part of me he touches caressingly, lovingly. Then he goes to my scalp, and I feel like I've died and gone to heaven. Whatever tension was there dissipates. A moan escapes, and I hear his chuckle rumble. Minutes, hours, days—I have no recollection of how long I've lain in this spot with this man touching everywhere on my body.

Ryker kneels in front of the couch, my head pointed toward him as my eyes flutter open. He's gorgeous, there is no mistaking it. It's what's in his eyes, though, that sends my heart into a tizzy. Compassion, understanding, caring, and yes—love. It hits hard, and he must see it on my face because he leans over and attaches his lips to mine.

The kiss becomes a passionate molding of two bodies as he lifts me. I straddle his lap on the floor as runs his hand through my hair before gripping it, but not painfully, more like guiding my head where he wants it. His lips are soft, yet they have a rough edge to them. Add in the friction of his beard on my face and it's a heady mixture.

Thoughts begin to swarm in my head, threatening to ruin this moment, but I push it all out—everything. Nothing else matters but Ryker and I in this moment. We have tonight, just he and I. No walls. No barriers. Just us.

Moving my mouth to match his, I do what feels natural, maneuvering my lips this way and that. My experience with men is very limited, and of that experience, this is the only time when I've felt beautiful, aroused, and in the moment.

My hips begin to move of their own accord, brushing back and forth along his hard length though his jeans. It hits a sensitive spot, and I gasp, loving the feel, only to keep doing it again, setting up a steady pace. This is so much more.

He cups my ass and squeezes, guiding my hips a bit faster.

Pulling away from his lips, my lungs take in much-needed oxygen as the build inside me grows. Ryker caresses his lips down my neck, darting his tongue out and licking me. I arch back for him, giving him more room, which he takes full advantage of, not leaving one space of flesh untouched.

He snakes one of his hands up my body so slowly it's almost like he's torturing me. The need for him to touch me more is so intense. He cups my breasts and begins to knead them, rolling my nipples repeatedly.

The room becomes hot like the desert in the middle of summer. Or maybe it's just me. My knees dig into the carpet and my thighs rub against his jeans, adding to the sensations. My underwear is damp, and need threatens to take me over.

Ryker finds my lips again. The kiss is wet and hot, scorching me from the inside-out. He moves his hands down my torso, under my shirt, and pulls it up, moving so agonizingly slow. Once he gets to my breasts, a bit of panic sets in that I have to breathe through. Then I lift my arms, and my shirt is gone.

Tonight is the night for all my firsts. The ones that matter.

"Damn, beautiful." He pulls down the cups of my dark purple lace bra, pulling my breasts out. The wire underneath holds them up, keeping them pert.

Ryker attaches his lips to my nipple, and I'm lost. The tugs, sucks, and nips bring me close. So close my core clenches and my head falls back on a loud moan. When he pulls away, I'm left on the cusp of what would be my first orgasm from a man.

"Why'd you stop?" My words are breathless. Hell, I don't even recognize them myself.

"Trust me."

A knot forms in my stomach for only a moment before I realize I've always trusted Ryker. Yes, he forced Deke's hand, but it wasn't because of anger. It was because he cared.

"Of course."

His answering smile is so sexy a whimper escapes me.

With my back to the couch, I lie back, giving him full access to my breasts as he goes back to giving each attention. He holds my hips still, and I take that as a sign to stop moving them, although I do love the friction.

"Wrap your legs around me tight," he says in a soft voice, and I comply.

Somehow, he rises, taking me with him and carrying me into my bedroom while kissing me sensuously. I thread my hands through his hair, loving the feel of its softness.

My back hits the bed, and then Ryker's weight comes on top of me.

"Waited for this for far too fuckin' long, beautiful. I'm takin' my time and gonna love every part of you."

My heart swells just as my insides melt. This is what I've wanted and dreamed of for so long it hurts. Now it's here and I'm taking in every second of it, burning it into my brain forever.

"Please," I answer.

Ryker makes a trail of his kisses down my neck, shoulder, chest, breasts, and down my torso. As he unzips my jeans, panic hits for a brief moment, but one look into his eyes and everything inside me calms and focuses on Ryker and his touch.

He pulls my jeans off, tossing them across the room. He then snakes his hands up my feet, legs, thighs, and hips. Ryker moves his head between my thighs, his mouth on my core. Well, on my underwear, but I can feel his heat pulsing off him as he massages my ass. My hips move of their own accord, back and forth, practically rubbing against his mouth.

On a chuckle, he pulls away, reaches up, and pulls my purple bikini briefs away from my body. I lie there, naked in front of him, the scars left over from JK on full display, as he stares down at me with a powerful gaze.

A shiver races through me. I know what I look like, and I like how I look, but Ryker's opinion of me matters. It probably shouldn't as much as it does, but it still does. I've grown to accept my scars. I just hope Ryker can, too.

I wait while he rests his hands on my thighs.

"You are absolutely the most gorgeous woman I've ever laid eyes on, Austyn. Always knew you'd be, but my visions didn't even come close to what's laying out in front of me."

The heart doesn't lie, they say. Mine is telling me that this man is more than I ever expected, too. More than the jokester façade. More than the brother to the Ravage MC. Behind it all is a man. A man who is capturing me with every touch he gives.

"Austyn," he calls, and my focus goes to him, not realizing my eyes were closed, lost in the moment. "There she is."

Ryker pulls off his T-shirt, tossing it somewhere in the room. My breath catches at the masculine beauty that is Ryker. I've seen him without his shirt on before at the clubhouse, but never this close. Never a time when I could look at him unabashedly and admire all that is him.

So many tattoos everywhere. I sit up onto my elbows, trying to take them all in, but there's no way it'll happen that quickly.

With a knee to the bed, he climbs on, kissing up my leg to my knee then to my pussy. I jolt at first, not having any clue what to expect. His tongue is hot and wet. His teeth are sharp and precise. He kisses me like he does my mouth, slow and sensually, making sure to hit my clit just at the right times to get a gasp from me. The brush of his hair down there amps up my arousal.

I reach down and hold onto his hair, my legs falling open and giving, which he takes full advantage of.

The pressure inside me coils, my stomach clenching. Heat like no other burns me from the inside out.

As he presses a finger inside me, the orgasm hits and I cry out Ryker's name while digging my nails in hard to his head. I'm not sure if I'm holding him there or trying to pull him off.

My entire body shakes, and my eyes roll shut as pleasure vibrates through my body.

Moments later, I look down to see Ryker's eyes are solely focused on me, taking in every little movement I make. He presses a kiss to the inside of my thigh, then rises from the bed, stripping off his jeans and boxers.

His cock stands to attention. It's long and thick with an almost purple head that looks like it could explode at any moment. I've seen men's junk before in movies, but Ryker's has every single one of those beat by a mile. I'm not even sure he'll fit inside me.

He pulls out a condom and tosses it to the bed before climbing up back on the bed. Then he delicately cups my face, kissing me with everything he has. The taste of myself mingled with him spurs my arousal on once again.

We roll to our sides, my leg over his thigh. His dick rubs against me as the fire burns hot once more.

"Like this?" I ask, fearing him being on top of me. Not him, just the feel of it. I don't want to ruin this. I can't ruin this.

"Anything," he says, kissing me once again.

I feel him moving, then feel his hand between us as he rolls the condom on.

A fleeting bit of panic hits, but I breathe through it, looking into Ryker's eyes.

This is Ryker. No one else.

The feeling subsides.

Ryker poises at my entrance. He knows I've had sex before because I was pregnant. What he doesn't know is he's my first time having sex.

His dick slowly enters me, and then he maneuvers my body for a better angle. He glides inside, each inch of him stretching me and waking up the nerves.

I try to hold back the tears, wishing this was my first time for real.

"Damn, baby. You're wrapping around me like a vise." Sweat trickles down his brow like it's almost painful for him to be taking such time with me, but I appreciate it more than he knows.

Clawing his shoulders as he enters me fully, I feel slight pain, but I'm able to hold in my reaction.

"This is the best fuckin' gift you could have given me."

Before I can respond, he's kissing me once more, all the while thrusting into me, his dick sliding in and out of me rhythmically. His kisses match his thrusts, and I get lost in the sensations.

I find myself moving with him, meeting him with each move. He holds me tightly to his body, his heat adding to my own, creating a combustible energy in the room.

Ryker swivels his hips, hitting my clit just in the right stop. I gasp, but Ryker just plunges deeper in my mouth.

He begins a pace with a thrust and a swivel, and I'm completely lost. I scream his name once again as shards of white light appear behind my lids, ripping my lips away from his, my back arching. He keeps me close to him, even as I dig my nails into his shoulders as his thrusts become more determined.

Soon, he buries his head in my shoulder, and I feel his dick twitch inside me. Our bodies still, the only sound is our labored breathing.

That wasn't fucking. That wasn't anywhere close to fucking.

What have I done?

There's no coming back from that.

None. There is no use in me even trying.

CHAPTER NINETEEN

RYKER

The daylight shines through the curtains as Austyn lies on my chest, sleeping soundly. Last night was better than I ever imagined. She's always been amazing in my eyes, but our compatibility and the sparks between us make us unstoppable.

The only thing that stands out is her hesitation with the actual act of sex. I watched her carefully as I slid inside her, and if I didn't know better, I'd swear she was about to cry. Yet, she didn't. It's not like I was her, but her actions left me a bit confused. After that initial entry, though, she was all in. We matched each other movement for movement.

Austyn is by far the best partner I've ever had. It's because I love her. I know it. I've never loved anyone the way I love her.

In the light of day, though, is she going to pull away again? Is she going to erect those fucking walls again? Is she going to push me away? Is she going to try to avoid me once again?

Nevertheless, I won't allow her to block me out. Not even for a moment. She's going to know exactly what it means to have a man love her. As if she didn't pick up on it the past few months.

She slowly stirs, her hand flexing on my chest. I wait to see her reaction, remaining still. She slowly lifts her head, her eyes sleepy from sex and lips beautifully puffy.

"Hey." Her voice is whispered and sexy.

"Hey, beautiful." I tuck a strand of loose hair behind her ear, and she sighs contently.

"Can we just pretend that it's still the night?"

I brush a kiss over her lips. "There's no reason to pretend. This is us—you and me. Not one damn other thing matters. This right here"—I pull her tighter to me—"is all that I give a shit about. You. Me. Us."

Tears well in her eyes, but she fights them back. "I wish it were that simple."

"It is. Just let it be." I lean down, kissing her hard and deeply, lying flat on the bed with her on top.

Her soft, compliant, still sleepy body molds to mine like a glove, fitting in the right places exactly. She kisses me with all the fervor of last night, meeting me at every turn and blowing my damn mind. Always knew she'd be sweet. Knew she'd be the one to wreck me. Having it confirmed only makes me harder.

Austyn rubs her pussy along the length of my bare cock, her knees on either side of my hips. The sensation drives me mad with desire, lust spiking through me.

Tilting her head, I take more, exploring every inch of her mouth with my tongue and lips. She's a fantastic kisser, so soft yet rough when she needs to be. Absolutely fucking perfect.

She lifts from my lips, her eyes dilated and breathing ragged as she continues to move over me.

"You're so fuckin' wet, beautiful."

Her glazed over look comes to me, her brunette hair falling around her like a curtain.

Reaching up, I grab her tits, needing the feel of her flesh. It's so soft, and it turns her on, if her hips going faster has anything to say about it. Tweaking each nipple, she cries out, tossing her head back. Her hair is so long it swipes over my legs, only adding to the sensations coursing through me.

I feel the pre-come leaking out of me and grasp her hips. "Beautiful, need to glove up and be inside that sexy body of yours." Reaching over, I grab the foil packet, tear it open, and glide it on.

She grasps my cock, and I have to hold in the urge to come because it rides me hard.

Poised at her entrance, she slowly lowers onto me. Her pussy is so damn tight she has to rock her hips back and forth inch by painful inch to let me in. Once her ass is resting on my hips, she stops, our eyes connecting.

Looking deeply within her, I see what I've been wanting to see, when her mouth kept telling me other things—love, compassion, and undying lust. They brew in her depths, wrapping around me like a winter scarf.

She brings her hands to my chest, palms flat, searing me with her heat. Blowing out a breath, sweat trickles down my face and chest. My patience is just about spent. Then she starts to move. Up and down, gliding along my shaft, her knees and legs working as one unit. The rhythm starts out uneven, but all too soon, she finds it.

Austyn drops her head back as a sexy as hell moan escapes her. I squeeze my hands on her hips, guiding her faster. My hips buck with each downward thrust from her. My cock is so deep inside I have to blink away the stars in my eyes.

"Oh, Ryker!" she calls out as our pace quickens.

I pop my feet flat on the bed, knees cocked up, and meet her each and every time. Her body falls to me, lips attaching to mine as she kisses and tries to breathe at the same time.

Wrapping my arms tightly around her back, I still her movements, taking her lips. I violently thrust my hips repeatedly, squeezing my ass muscles, trying to make my cock penetrate further.

Holding her immobile, her lips fall from mine as she moves her face to my neck. I continue to hammer into her.

Austyn's wetness is heard throughout the room, along with her pants, mewls, and cries.

Her pussy walls contract around my cock, making the slide in and out more difficult but so much better.

"Ryker!" she screams loud enough to shake the walls of the room. Only then do I allow my cock to burst inside her. The muscles in my abs jump with each squirt of my release until everything is spent.

Austyn's body relaxes into mine, her breathing matching my very own. Sweat coats both our skin. I reach up, cradling the back of her neck, and pull her lips to mine.

This is exactly what I want to wake up to every fucking morning of my life.

Yes, I'm ruined.

"You're going to cook?" Austyn asks with a genuine smile on her face. One I've been getting a lot of since our excursion the other day. Each time she gives me one is a gift. Ones I take greedily.

Pulling out a pot and setting it on the stove, I tell her, "Yep. The one thing I remember from my mother's cooking is hamburger, peppers, and cheese. You can't go wrong with it."

She leans against the doorframe, happiness radiating from her. "Sounds good. Do you want help?"

"Sure. Chop up the peppers."

She enters the kitchen, stopping next to me, and we spend the next few hours cooking, eating, and laughing.

There's a fight in her eyes that she tries to hide. One that wants to let everything go, yet she still finds herself holding back. Lately, though, she's been able to let loose and be with me. That's another one of her gifts, only making me love her more.

My cell rings, the screen reading, *Mom calling.*

I lean down to Austyn. "Gotta take this."

She moves off my lap and sits up on the couch. Then I make my way to the balcony with the door open and light a smoke.

"Yeah?"

"Matthew?" The voice is hushed, so much so I can't make out who it is.

"Who is this?"

There's a hesitation, then, "It's Breanna."

I inhale deeply. This can't be good.

"Samantha told me to call you," she continues.

I'm hoping this is a call to get her out of that house. I was going to do it on my own. Just, with Austyn, I haven't been focusing on it. I need to. This is my wakeup call. I need to pay more attention.

"Okay," I lead, trying to get her to tell me what she wants. If she doesn't want to leave, then it won't matter because she'll just go back. I've always assumed she didn't want to be in that life, but I could be far off the mark.

"Samantha said you were going to get her out."

"Yes." I have to keep reminding myself she's only fifteen, almost sixteen, but fuck, it's like pulling teeth to get her to talk. She's also socially awkward, being so sheltered her entire life. It's another thing I have to keep in mind.

"Dad had me meet with William today."

Bile rises up my throat. William is the *leader*, if that's the correct term nowadays. He's the one who determines your spouse match.

"He has men picked out for me, and I just can't ..." She trails off, and then I hear her soft crying on the other end of the phone.

"Tell me what you need, Breanna," I prompt, hoping she comes out and says it. I try not to let the anger show through, afraid I might scare her.

"I want out. I don't want to marry those men. Two are my cousins, and one is my half-brother. That's just icky, Matthew." *Icky*. It reminds me of how sheltered my siblings are from the outside world. She may be going on sixteen, but she's much younger than that socially.

"Alright. When do you want me to get you?"

"Just like that?" She sounds surprised, but she should know I mean business from Samantha. No way I'll let her stay in that place if she doesn't want to be there. My thoughts are, if William and James think she's old enough to be picking out a potential husband to be with for the rest of her life, then she's completely capable of making the decision that she doesn't want to be in that life.

"Yep. What's the plan?"

"I ..." She hesitates. I forgot again that I need to walk her through it.

"When will Mom and the kids be gone while you're at home? Or would you be able to leave at school?"

"Not at school; too many people. It has to be at the house and with dark cover. Either while everyone's sleeping or when Mom goes to church tomorrow night."

There's only one option there. "When Mom goes to church."

"I'm supposed to watch all the kids."

Fuck.

"So, they'll be there then?" *Shit.*

"Yeah."

Okay, change in plans.

"Here's the deal, since the kids are home, let's do it while everyone's sleeping. That'll be better than the first."

"Okay."

"Tomorrow night, one in the morning, I'll be waiting outside the back left window to the basement. You're going to crawl through the window, and then we're out of there. Got it?"

"I'm scared. If she catches us ..."

"It won't happen, and even if it does, I'm not the same little boy I was when I left. We're doing this quietly, so I don't jolt the neighbors and they start making phone calls, then I have a mob or cops on my hands. Quick and quiet."

"Okay."

"You only pack what you need in a duffle bag. One. Don't bring curling irons and shit like that. Only bring clothes and personal things that you can't get at a store. Don't start packing until everyone goes to bed tomorrow. That way, no one will catch you and ask what you're doing."

"Okay."

"Are you okay?" I ask when she says nothing else and the dead air takes over.

"Yeah, I'm just scared, but I can't do it. I have to leave."

"You leave, that means no contact with the other siblings or Mom. You're on your own, but I'll help you get all set up."

She sniffles. "I know."

"Alright. I'll be there tomorrow at one a.m. Be ready."

"Thank you." She clicks off the phone just as Austyn comes out to stand by me on the balcony.

"What's going on?" she asks, leaning her elbows on the wrought iron railing.

Ripping my other hand through my hair, I answer, "We're gonna go get my sister tomorrow night. She wants to leave."

"Samantha?"

"No, Breanna. She turns sixteen soon, and they already have matches for her. Two are her cousins, and one is a half-brother. It's not fuckin' happenin'." I toss out the smoke. "We need to head over to the clubhouse."

She nods.

For this, I'll need my brothers at my back.

"Let's do this." I glance over at Austyn. "You ready."

"Not like I'm doing much but sitting in the truck, waiting for them to jump in. I'm sure I can hack it."

Reaching over, I wrap my hand around the back of her neck and pull her lips to mine for a quick kiss.

"Can y'all not do that in front of me?" Nox whines, but I don't give a fuck. We haven't been around the guys since our relationship turned. Nevertheless, I make no apologies for kissing my woman. *Fuck that.*

"Shut it," I order with a smile. "There shouldn't be any trouble. I'll be in and out quickly. We just gotta watch the neighbors."

"Tell me again why we don't just break down the fuckin' door and take her out?" Rhys chimes in.

"We're tryin' to make her disappear. If they know I had anything to do with it, they'll sick the cops on me so fast my head'll spin. The cops are one of *them* around here and will have no trouble bouncing us all behind bars. Not only that, they'll send out the lynch mob beforehand, and the less bodies we have to deal with, the better. We want a clean in and out."

"Fuckin' idiots," Rhys grumbles, walking back to his truck. No bikes this time; too loud for the neighborhood.

GT clamps a hand on my shoulder. "Let's get her out and get the fuck out of here. This place is fuckin' twisted."

"You're telling me." I look down at my watch. "Ten minutes. I'll radio if there are any problems. Only then do you move in."

"Got it, Captain," Deke teases, but not in a fun way. He's still pissed about his hand being forced. What he needs to remember is he's still a fucking prospect.

Not having time to deal with it, I kiss Austyn one more time then shut the door.

Everyone leaves while I wait. Those ten minutes seem to take for-fucking-ever. Like the second hand on the clock doesn't want to move correctly. The house has no lights on, but two lights outside illuminate a lot of the space, so we'll easily be seen.

There are two cars in the driveway, both empty. The neighbor has one light on, but it looks like it's over a kitchen sink. That could possibly be one that's on all the time, yet I don't know for sure. The other neighbor's house is dark. Even with them dark, my alertness is on high, making sure that all is clear.

My watch finally shows one o'clock. Austyn gives me a nod, and then I'm off, creeping through this little town like a thief in the night. Down the sidewalks and through the driveway. A dog barks in the distance, and I'm hoping it isn't close. That's the last thing I need.

Going around the back side of the house, I find the left window is open with no screen on it. At least she's really ready to come with me.

"Breanna?" I whisper into the night.

Nothing.

Fuck, maybe she chickened out.

I wait, looking in the window and seeing nothing but darkness inside. Time starts to tick by. It's funny how fast it goes when you want it to slow down.

"Breanna?" Poking my head in, I see movement off to the side. "Breanna?"

"Yeah, hang on." She's rummaging through something, which she should have done before I got here.

"We don't have time to hang on. Move!"

"Okay," she whisper-yells. "Be quiet; Dad's here tonight."

"You're fuckin' shittin' me." Of all the times for that motherfucker to show up, it has to be when I'm here and taking one of his prized girls. He covets the girls like expensive money because they are the ones who keep this lifestyle going. *Stupid fucker.*

"No. Now move." She tosses a duffle bag out of the window opening, then tosses a second.

"Now," Breanna says, and then a small body comes out of the window. *Holy fuck.*

"Breanna, what are you doing?"

"I'm not leaving her behind. She only has a few more years, then she'll be in my shoes. She's the last girl," she says hastily, climbing out the window behind our younger sister Ashley.

My heart thumps loudly. This isn't what I planned. Not two minors who now need places to escape. *Fuck me.*

A loud shatter comes from the window, one of the panes lays on the ground in pieces. Lights come on. There is no time to argue.

"Go. Down the road to the left until you get to the black truck. Get inside."

I grab both the duffle bags, and then we head out around the side. The front porch light comes on as we get there.

"Go to the truck."

Breanna stops. "He'll be mad."

"Fuckin' go!" I yell just as the front door swings open with such force it hits the side of the house. My sperm donor comes out, wearing pajama pants and a T-shirt with *"He's the one"* on the front. *Asshole.*

"What's going on here?" James asks, quickly coming down the stairs and directly toward me on bare feet. Holding my ground, my feet stay planted as he approaches. "Who are you and what do you want?" he demands like he's some sort of king or some shit and I'm supposed to listen to his bullshit. No, not happening.

He's pudgier than I remember, and his dark hair has turned gray. His eyes show years of keeping secrets and how they are paying a toll on him now.

"Hey, Daddy-o. Remember me?"

He blinks repeatedly, looking me up and down. When it clicks in his head, his mouth turns in disgust. "Matthew?"

"The one and only. Seems you have a problem that I'm takin' care of."

He lifts his chin with confidence. "And what's that?"

I lean in. "Two girls who want nothing to do with this life."

His eyes round. "Charlotte, check the girls! What did you do to them?" His face turns a vibrant shade of red, and even with it dark, the glow from the light accentuates it. It's not a good color for him at all. With his yelling, though, he's going to draw attention and fast. That's what he wants. He wants his minions to come out and get in my face. *Idiot.*

"They're gone!" my mother wails, running out the door. "Matthew, what are you doing?"

"The girls want to come with me. I'm takin' them somewhere safe where you can't find them … ever." I press the button on my walkie, knowing my brothers will be there momentarily. "James, I have enough information gathered on you to sink your entire operation. To close your banks and your stores—everything. Gone in a puff of smoke."

I sense my brothers behind me, but it's my sperm donor's round eyes that tell me for a fact.

"See these men behind me? They're my family. We protect each other with everything we have. You come after me or those girls, we'll end all of this and you'll have nothing left."

Truth be told, I don't have information that would destroy their operation, but that doesn't mean I can't get it. It's a bluff I'm rolling with, seeing if he'll take the bait.

"You can't do this!" James exclaims.

"Please don't," my mother pleads, tears streaming down her face.

"She already has her future husbands lined up. Two cousins and a half-brother. Nice. That's fuckin' nasty. You look at me with disgust, but that's where you're wrong. *You* disgust *me*."

"I don't really care what you think of me. God has told me what He wants of me, and I'm following His rules."

"Bullshit. You wouldn't know the truth if it bit you on the ass."

"Brother, we need to go," GT says from my side. That's when I notice more lights coming on in the neighborhood. We killed the cameras on the road, so at least they won't show us here.

"We're leaving. Don't come anywhere near us or you'll be done for. Not only will I get your ass thrown in jail for your underage activities, I'll destroy you. Think of this as my revenge." On those parting words, I turn to my brothers, nodding, and then we all take off like shots.

I hear footfalls behind me, having no doubt it's my sperm donor.

Girls are such a high commodity in this world, he'll do anything to keep them. Anything.

Turning around, I find he's only a few beats behind me. I jump into an already running truck—thank you, Austyn—and we take off into the night.

In the rearview mirror, I see my father stomping his feet and waving his hands in the air, angry as all hell.

I'm going to need to find these two somewhere to go, now.

"Are you okay?" I ask the girls, who are crying in the backseat of my extended cab.

Breanna sniffles. "We'll be fine. We just have to get out of here."

Austyn reaches over and grabs my hand, giving it a squeeze. "I'll call Mom."

I nod, thanking Christ that Princess has connections.

CHAPTER TWENTY

Austyn

The girls are petrified. I don't blame them one bit. They don't know me and trying to talk to them is like pulling teeth. Ryker said they don't have very good social skills, which scares me. They need to be able to stand on their own two feet, but I fear they won't be able to. Hopefully, wherever my mom has in store will help them get to that point in their lives.

"Yeah?" Mom answers on the first ring.

Looking out into the dark night, I tell her, "We have a situation."

"Talk to me." Her tone becomes alert instantly. That's her sign for she's all business.

"We have two girls. Breanna, who's fifteen and …" I look to Ryker, not knowing the other one's name or age.

"Ashley." He looks back to the little girl.

"Eleven." Her soft voice comes through a bit shaken.

I go back to the phone. "Ashley, who's eleven. We need a place for them tonight."

"Fuck." She shuffles around. "Alright. Give me ten, and I'll call you right back." She disconnects.

"Call your dad for me," Ryker says.

I dial then hand him the phone.

"Yeah. We have two girls, both my full-sisters. One's fifteen, the other eleven. Princess is working on a place for them to go. We need them to disappear, and I don't want to bring them to the clubhouse. Our father was outside and saw me ... saw all of Ravage, actually. I threatened him, but I don't know if it'll work. The best bet is to find them a place now. Princess is workin' on it."

I don't hear what my father says, and it makes me want to push speaker so I can.

"I'm going to head west. You and Princess tell us where we're goin'." A pause. "Right. Bye."

Ryker looks over to me. "Looks like we're goin' on a road trip."

My head falls back to the seat. I didn't bring my laptop with me, and I just feel like it's getting close to when JK fucks up. This isn't good.

Ten minutes later, the phone rings and I answer my mom's call. "Hello?"

"Alright. My guy can do it. Five a.m. in Stalemont, at the corner of Parish and Crest. Xavier and his wife Kim will be there. You give them the code. Tell the girls to go with him, and he'll make them disappear."

I search my memory, and it hits me. This churns in my gut. Ryker just got his sisters back, and now he's going to lose them again.

"Right. Can Ryker know where they're going?'

"No. It'll be a while for that, but I trust these people, Austyn. They will take care of the girls. Swear it.”

I lean my head back on a huff of air. I may not like this, but it’s the best way to go about it. My mom has never let me down, and I know she won’t start now.

“Right. We’ll be there.”

Clicking off the phone, I give Ryker the details, telling him the sad news. He already knew it would be like this and is rolling with it.

“I just want them safe,” is all he says.

My heart grows for this man for taking care of sisters he barely knows. He has so much love inside him. I ache for the little boy who lost his family so early in life. Not by choice, but because he was made to. Breanna and Ashley had a choice on what to do; Ryker didn’t, and that hurts.

Part of me wants to hold and shelter him from all this bullshit. It must suck, coming all back up to the surface and slapping him in the face. All I can do right now is reach over and hold his hand, giving him my strength and telling him that he’s not alone.

I try again to talk to the girls, but they look like terrified little rabbits and don’t respond back, just look at me with doe eyes. I’m just hoping that Kim and Xavier have better luck getting through to them.

All too soon, we are slowing down at the drop-off point. Ryker puts the truck in park, shutting down the lights.

“You’re going to go with some friends of ours. Ones we trust to take care of you and keep you safe.” Ryker pulls out a disposable phone and hands it to Breanna. “Only one number you can call on this, and it’s me. Only call if it’s an absolute emergency, do you understand?”

Her face is red and puffy. “Yeah.” She pauses. “Thank you. I’m scared. Very scared, but Samantha was trusting you, and I am, too.”

"Right," Ryker says, opening the door to the truck, then opening the back door. I follow suit.

A black Tahoe awaits us, both doors open. A man with dark jet-black hair and a mustache to match comes forward. He has an edge to him that's a little scary, and I've lived with bikers my whole life. Kim comes around the other side. She has long blonde hair and a killer smile.

"Hi, I'm Kim," she says with a grin. "And this is Xavier."

"Hi. Ryker, Austyn," Ryker introduces.

"Sure is a good day to go on a Cruz," Xavier says, looking us dead in the eye.

I answer, "Yeah, my friend Princess loves to go on them." This passcode was given to my brothers and I when we were little. My mom said if she ever had someone pick us up from school, that was the code. We haven't used it in years.

A smile comes over his face. "Yes, that woman is something."

"She's my mom," I tell him.

His smile widens. "No shit?"

I nod.

Ryker steps forward. "These are my sisters. They haven't been out around a lot of people, so please be patient with them."

"That's not a problem," Kim responds, looking at the girls. "Hi, girls. I'm Kim, and we're gonna get out of here, okay?"

Breanna nods and pulls Ashley along while Ryker hands Xavier the bags.

"Be safe," Ryker tells them, and before we can blink, they are gone.

I'm not sure what I expected, maybe a hug between them or a thank you. I don't know, but whatever it was, it didn't happen.

We head back to the truck, a somber feeling settling in the cab, but there's also a little bit of triumph. Ryker holds my hand most of the way home.

Entering the apartment with the early morning light among us, we find Emery sitting in the recliner.

"What's going on?" she asks.

"We're good," I tell her, then lead Ryker into the bedroom.

Ryker is hanging in there, though the sadness around him is like a dark cloud.

Locking the door, I tell him, "Let's get some sleep."

Methodically, we strip our clothes and climb into bed. I wrap myself around Ryker, and he does the same to me, then kisses the top of my head.

It's quiet in the room. I focus on our in sync breathing.

"It's strange," he cuts through the silence of the dark room with only the alarm clock's light casting a very soft shade of red. "I'm happy they got out, but I worry about them. They're with someone they don't know, and you saw how scared they were. I fucking hate they were exposed to that shit." Ryker squeezes me tightly. "It's just bringing up old shit I buried a long time ago."

Hand on his chest, I say, "Tell me."

He blows out a deep breath, his chest moving my head, but he doesn't release me, thankfully. "They kicked me out because I asked too many questions about their lifestyle. I didn't think what was happening was right. It sounded twisted and weird to me. Even being raised in that world, it felt odd.

"James didn't like anyone challenging his idealizations. The more questions I asked, the angrier he got. When he got angry, I got a cheap thrill from it. I thought it meant I was on to something. Which I was.

When they put me out, I had nothing. Dumpster diving was my only means for food. Lived on the streets. Shit sucked, and I had to learn to deal with my mother allowing him to put me out and trying to get my head on straight. It was a lot to take on."

"But you survived."

He scoffs. "It took me a fuck of a long time to get where I am today, Austyn. Stealing. Begging. It wasn't pretty, but it's how I got to here. I just don't want my sisters to feel the way I did. Abandoned. Alone. Helpless."

"If my mom says that Kim and Xavier will take care of them, they will. You don't have to worry about that."

He kisses my head again. "I know that, beautiful. It just fucks up your head. The whole lifestyle. Coming out of it. All of it together is a lot for anyone to handle. Ashley is so young. I just hope she can hack it."

He sighs deeply. "My cousin Carley, the one you saw on the back of my bike, she got out on her own. Ran away, actually, and didn't come and find me until a year or so afterward. She had a hell of a time adjusting to life outside. They keep you so sheltered socially that surviving in the world is difficult, but Carley did it. She has her own place and a job outside of Sumner as a bank teller. I'm just hoping my sisters can adjust that well."

I feel his pain. I wouldn't want Nox or Cooper to feel anything like this. It would crush me deeply. The need to make it disappear for him hits me hard.

Rolling over, I touch my lips to his as I straddle his body, roaming my hands over him. "Let me take it away."

He kisses me, teeth clashing, each trying to get more and more from each other. The kiss is bruising. I've never felt so desired in my life. The thought that he wants me so badly he can't contain himself sends me into an arousal that's more intense, which I didn't think was possible.

Breaking away from his lips, I trail kisses down his neck, his chest, and his abs, loving the way they jolt by my touch. His cock is right there, hard and ready. Nerves hit me in a rush, and it takes me a moment to pull myself together and push it all away. Yes, he's been inside me and I've touched him, but I've never come face to face with this part of a man.

Just doing what comes naturally to me, I grip him hard, to which he sucks in a breath. *Here goes nothing and everything.*

I latch my mouth around his hardness that feels soft against my lips.

"Oh, fuck!" he calls out, fisting the sheets next to us.

I take him in as far as I can, feeling the urge to gag. Remembering a video I saw once with a woman going down on a guy, I recall her licking around the head, dipping into the small slit. Doing exactly what she did in the video causes Ryker to growl, telling me it was the right thing to do.

He leaks out, and I swipe it, then swallow it down. It tastes a bit salty, which I like.

Wrapping around him, moving up and down, my movements become erratic as my own arousal hits hard. I reach under myself and find my clit, rubbing it hard and fast.

"Oh no, you don't." Ryker pulls me away from his cock and smiles when I frown.

"I wasn't done yet."

He flips me over onto my back. "Yeah, you are, because I'm coming inside your hot pussy."

Ryker pulls out a condom and sheathes himself, the reflection of the small light illumining his movements. He lifts my leg high, almost to my ear, bending at the knee. Then he's inside me.

There is no playing this time. No waiting ever so slowly for him to enter me. No, he impales me so deeply my back arches off the bed with only his weight holding me down, my breasts pressed against his chest.

A noise comes from my lips that I don't recognize. In this position, new nerves and feelings arise in my core and his dick rubs a spot right at the top of my walls. Over and over he hits that one place inside me, and I lose myself, eyes closing. My core clenches, sending heat and shocks of electricity all throughout my body.

Ryker doesn't stop as I ride out my orgasm.

"Fuck!" he calls out as he comes inside me on a growl, stilling and letting pleasure take him over. Then he falls to the side of me, his cock slipping out as he moves. He pulls me into his arms, wrapping warmth and security around me as we fall asleep.

I groan as the phone rings. Looking at the clock, I see we've only gotten a couple hours of sleep, reminding me I need to text Lexa and tell her I'm not coming in today. Standing on my feet all day isn't an option right now.

Ryker reaches over and tags his phone. "Yeah?" His body jolts, signaling sleep time is over. "You're fuckin' shittin' me?" He sits up, rolls out of bed, and begins to get dressed, holding the phone between his shoulder and ear the entire time.

Begrudgingly, I follow suit.

"Be there in ten." Hanging up, he looks to me. "My sperm donor called it into the police. We have thirty-five minutes to get to the clubhouse before they arrive."

"Shit."

"Yeah, that motherfucker is going to regret he ever touched the Ravage MC. Fuckin' warned him. Now he's going to feel it."

With the anger coming off Ryker, there isn't a doubt in my mind he's telling the truth. And once someone fucks with Ravage, it's all hands on deck.

CHAPTER TWENTY-ONE

Austyn

Bursting through the doors of the clubhouse, I find Buzz waiting for me.

"Got the call from a buddy of mine at our local. Asshole reported it last night, but the tapes were already wiped, so there's no proof any of us were there. They're just coming to question and wanted to do it here."

"Fuckin' dickhead. He doesn't think I or the Ravage MC have any power. That we are nothing in his precious, little, sick, twisted life. We're gonna show him we do."

Buzz smiles sadistically. It's almost as frightening as when Rhys gets ahold of someone he doesn't like. Except, Buzz's is all about the computers.

"Everything you can dig up on, him. I'll do what I can on my end. Let's wipe this fuckin' guy and his entire operation off the fuckin' grid.

Everything crushed and destroyed. We gotta make shit up, that's what we do. I don't give a flying fuck at this point. He's done." Only the slightest of hesitations hits me, and that's related to my mother and siblings still there. If we destroy everything, it will make her in need of more help, but I'll figure that out later.

"On it." Buzz takes off down the stairs to his technology lair. He'll have most of it done before I finish with the cops, unless we have to call in some favors to get something finalized.

"What do you want me to do?" Austyn asks, her hand on my chest, looking like she'd move the world for me if she could. Fuck, it's beautiful.

"You bein' here, beautiful."

She gives me a huge smile and sags into me. I wrap my arm around her waist.

Princess shows up from around the corner. "Come help me make some food."

Austyn looks up at me, and I pull her up for a kiss.

"Go ahead."

"Right." She gives me a squeeze then goes off with her mother.

I sit with Tug, Cooper, Nox, Green, and a few others.

"Takin' good care of my sister?" Nox asks with an intense stare.

"What do you think?"

"Finally got in there, huh?" Cooper adds.

"Can we get off my love life, assholes?"

They both smile, letting me know they're just giving me shit. While it feels good, having the cops here boils my blood. Seeking my ultimate revenge will be worth it. I'll wipe the world of those assholes once and for all.

A banging comes to the door.

"Let me handle this shit. Asshole's gonna pin it on me."

Sure enough, the cops are all over my ass, but have zero proof and can't do shit to me. There aren't any other witnesses besides James and my mother. No one to collaborate their story.

James is going to know what it's like to get shit on. Fucking piece of shit is going down.

Afterward, I search the clubhouse, looking for Austyn and running into her mom.

"You know where Austyn is?"

Her eyes grow intense like she's going to throw the hammer down on me and nail me to the fucking wall. This should be good.

Even I have to admit Princess is a badass motherfucker. She's one woman you do not want to meet in a dark alley with her pissed off at you. She's the one you want to have your back in that alley.

"Ya know," she starts, crossing her arms over her chest, "always knew my girl loved you. You better not hurt her, Ryker. I'll slice off your balls."

I feel my nads shrivel up a bit. I've heard stories about how Princess deals with men who fuck her over. Once, she ripped a guy's balls so hard away from his body he sure as shit will never have kids.

"Gotcha."

"Are you threatening again?" Cruz comes up to his wife and wraps an arm around her shoulders.

"Just makin' sure Ryker here knows what it's like to be in the family."

I can't help the smile that graces my face, taking that as their approval.

"Right. She's downstairs with some of the kids."

"Right. Thanks."

I jet off down the stairs and into the basement. It was redone years ago to be more of a kid zone. Most of the time, the kids are just watching movies or playing one of the arcade games Tug insisted on getting. Not that I'll complain. Skee-ball is fun as hell, but Pac-Man can suck my dick.

Getting to the bottom of the stairs, I see Austyn sitting on the L-shaped couch with only Mazie, Tanner and Rhys's youngest daughter. Some movie is playing where they are singing about being wicked and the two girls have blue and purple hair.

"Whatcha watchin'?" I ask, moving next to the couch.

Austyn smiles up at me.

"*Descendants 2*!" Mazie says excitedly. "It's just started. Ryker, come sit with us!"

"I don't think so." The singing and dancing on the screen is officially freaking me the fuck out.

Austyn grabs my hand, giving it a squeeze, but it's Mazie who talks.

"It's awesome. It has pirates and kings! You have to! Plllleaaasse!"

I move to the front of the couch and sit next to Austyn, pulling her to me. "I can't say no to a pretty girl."

Mazie beams while Austyn elbows me in the ribs. On an *oomph*, a chuckle leaves me.

"What?"

"You'd better be saying no to all the girls, mister."

She sets me on fire.

I lean down to her ear. "You're all I want and all I need, beautiful."

"*Hello*! The movie is on!" Mazie says, bouncing up on the couch

210

and trying to get our attention.

After placing a small peck on Austyn's lips, I say, "Alright, tell me what this is about."

Mazie doesn't answer, already too enthralled in the movie.

There's a cauldron, apples, and four kids singing about being wicked, then dancing all over a school. Lord help me if this is what this whole thing is about.

Two hours later, the movie spins in my head like a bad dream. *Holy fuck.* I lost count the number of songs they sang and danced, but fuck, it was a lot. Little purple-haired girl thought she was badass. Then the pirate girl ... fuck, she was some octopus or something. Hell, if I know. I would much rather get shot in every limb of my body than watch that movie again.

There's one part in it, though, that got me. So much so Austyn saw it during the moving yet said nothing.

"Wasn't it great?" Mazie says with an amazement I won't dare squash.

Standing up from the couch, I stretch out my arms, my shirt rising just a bit. "It was interesting."

"I know! I just love it. I've watched it so many times, and I'm trying to learn all the words to the songs. Oh, and the dances! That would be so cool!" Mazie leans over to Austyn. "Thank you for watching it with me. Dad says, if he has to watch it again, he's going to bleach his eyeballs."

This makes me laugh. That totally sounds like something Rhys would say.

"Anytime, but we've gotta get goin' now."

Austyn rises from the couch just as two little arms wrap around my waist, her head right at my abs.

"Thank you, Ryker." Mazie then bounces off.

"She's somethin'."

Austyn comes closer and steps right into my arms with zero hesitation. Fucking love that. "Yeah, she reminds me of me when I was little. I used to love these movies, and my parents would get fed up about the tenth time I watched one." She pauses. "How did it go?"

Brushing her hair away from her face, I then cup her cheek. "They just questioned me. It's his and my mother's word against mine. It won't go anywhere."

"Are you sure? I mean, they're minors. I don't want you to …" She trails off. I know what she's thinking.

"Nothing's going to happen to me." I kiss her deeply, then pull away. "But, he will pay."

She nods, not asking any questions. Another reason we fit so damn well together. She understands that there are some things I can't talk to her about.

Damn, I love this woman.

"Okay." She pauses, and I feel it coming. "What about that part in the movie when you tensed up?"

Letting out a deep breath, I tell her, "It was the part where the pirate, teal-haired chick talked about the lost boys and girls. That's what I was called once they kicked me out. A lost boy. Dealing with all this is just dredging up all sorts of shit that was locked down."

"Why did they call you that?"

I tightly squeeze her as I answer, "Because that's what we are. We're lost to them. Don't exist."

"You said boys and girls?"

"Nah, the girls were just in that movie. It's only the boys who get kicked out. My cousin Carley, she chose to leave, and that's really the only way she could've gotten out. They won't risk losing the girls."

Her eyes shine with sadness. "I'm sorry."

"I'm not. My life had to happen the way it did to end up in this spot, right here with you. No way would I do anything to fuck that up." Leaning down, I take her mouth. "Let's go up." I hold her hand the entire way up.

As soon as we hit the top, Rhys bursts out laughing. "Fuckin' suckers!"

"It wasn't bad," Austyn says, not letting go of my hand.

Rhys only laughs harder, this time with his head thrown back. "Love my baby girl, but fuck me. If I have to see those pirates dancin' around one more time, I'm burnin' that DVD."

"You can't burn it, Dad. It's on Prime," Mazie says, approaching her dad.

Rhys pulls his daughter onto his lap. "Then I'll bust all the tablets."

Mazie's eyes grow round. "What? Daddy, no!"

The smile never leaves his face. That man loves his girls with everything he has. He has another one, Rylynn. I'm not sure where she is.

Austyn curls into me, her head tilted up to me, eyes gleaming with humor and lust. It's a beautiful look on her. Not thinking twice, I lean down and take her lips roughly. She gives in, fully pressing her body against mine like glue.

When hoots and hollers come from the peanut gallery, we break apart, but all I notice is the smile on Austyn's face.

"I've thought of this exact thing." Her voice is soft.

"What, me kissin' you? 'Cause, baby, that's gonna happen a lot."

She slaps her hand over my chest playfully. "No. My parents. My father doesn't hold back when he kisses my mother. He doesn't care who's around or what they think. He does what he wants."

"Beautiful, I'm not sure where you're going with this, but talkin' about your parents while my dick is hard as a rock isn't top on my list."

"Oh, zip it and listen."

I close my mouth with a grin.

"I always told myself that I would be with a guy like that. One who didn't care who was around. One who loved me enough to show the world that I was his and he was mine. A man who took as much as he gave. A man who treated me the same way I've seen my dad treat my mom over the years." Her eyes beam. "And you've given me that. Thank you."

Fuck. My chest tightens to the point of pain, but it's a gorgeous pain, one I never want to stop. It's like an unbreakable bond is connecting right before my eyes. One that won't waver and won't be broken. I hope to Christ she feels the same way.

"Beautiful, I'll give you anything and everything I got."

"Alright. As happy as I am for you two," Cruz says, slapping me on the shoulder, "you even attempt to take this further in my presence, I'll beat the fuck out of you."

Austyn lets out a laugh, tightly holding me.

Finally, she's let me in fully. Time to get the fuck out of here and show her how much I love her.

CHAPTER TWENTY-TWO

Austyn

My body is sweaty and well-used. Work was slow, so I went home early and decided the gym was in order. It was pretty busy today. It took me a bit to get through my routine, Ryker helping me along the way. With each punch and kick, I imagined it was JK's body I was attacking. If nothing else, it made me feel better. That's what matters. Not that I was feeling horrible, but I've been feeling off lately.

The last week and a half has been fantastic with Ryker. I've allowed myself to open up more and show him exactly what he gets with me. So far, he's loved it all. At least, that's what he says.

I found out that trying to push him away took way too much energy—his pull is very strong. It's so much easier to let things happen, and so far, it's been spectacular. He's my man, and I'm his woman; I've learned to accept that. Furthermore, he knows all about my past. It's like a dream come true.

The only downfall to us being so tight is I've had to sneak into the bathroom to check my computer for information. That means my bathroom time has been a bit long, and considering Emery asked me *is everything coming out okay*, I knew I had to chill with it.

This doesn't make me happy. JK is a sneaky fuck. I want to watch the feeds and see if the emails have come or gone, and if they have, I want to see if the worm is doing its job.

Losing my focus on JK is not what I want. I've come too far to lose it now, but it's hard when the man you've craved lies next to you every night.

Not only do I want vengeance, he needs to be silenced forever. Just thinking about JK opening his mouth sends me into a downward spiral that I can't afford. No, he's not worth that. I'll find him, and it'll go away. It must, because it will ruin everything Ryker and I have built.

"What are ya thinkin' so hard about, beautiful?"

I shrug, pulling my legs up onto the couch. "My mind just wanders sometimes."

Ryker hauls me over to his side, putting his arm around me. "You need to talk, I'm here. I don't give a fuck what it's about. No more of this shit eatin' at you. It's done, and now we deal with it together."

As the guilt hits me hard, I lean over and kiss him roughly, telling him everything in my kiss while wiping my mind free of the "what-ifs."

He pulls me onto his lap, tightly gripping my ass before ripping his lips away. "Clothes. Off. Now." His words are choppy as desire swarms in his eyes.

Getting up, I remove everything as Ryker pulls out his cock from his jeans and begins to stroke it while watching me. That is so damn hot.

Ryker then drops his ass to the floor, his back to the couch. "Come sit on my face."

Puzzlement fills me on how to complete this task, but Ryker doesn't give me a chance to think. He tugs me forward then lifts my ass so my knees go on either side of his head. My hands reflexively fall to the back of the couch. Then his lips are on me—hot, wet, and so damn good.

He grips my thighs, but I still manage to move my hips, matching his rhythm and feeling the slow burn creep inside me. He kisses my core like he does when he kisses my lips, like he can't get enough of me.

"Oh, God! Ryker!" I scream out as he hits a very sensitive spot, almost putting me over the edge. He devours me, tasting, sucking, and nipping.

"Ride it," he growls, and just like riding a motorcycle, I do, swirling my hips and grinding myself down on his face.

His tongue spears inside me, sending pleasure spiking. Ryker continues his assault on my pussy.

"Right there. Right there!" I yell out as he touches that spot once more, causing pleasure to streak through me.

I clutch the couch, holding on for dear life, as my head shakes back and forth, my hair going everywhere.

He rides me out until my body goes limp. Then, without warning, he's up and pushing me down so I'm on my hands and knees. Ryker is behind me, his hard length rubbing up and down my already sensitive core. There's movement for a moment, then tearing noise, and then he's inside me.

I fall to my elbows as his thrusts become so powerful I can't hold myself up. With my back arched, the penetration is deep. And with him

217

behind me, holding my hips, it's rough.

I move backward as he moves forward, my body flushed and more aroused by the moment. In this moment, I realize how strong Ryker is and how much power he controls around me. This isn't the sweet love we made the first time. No, this is raw, carnal fucking. Two bodies searching for a release that will block out time.

With the history bestowed upon me, I never thought this could be a part of my life—this desperate need for someone—but here it is, in all its bold colors, ready to paint my world into a beautiful mural.

In and out, over and over, his hands digging so deeply into my hips I know I'll have bruises, and I don't care one bit.

The pressure inside me builds, my eyes rolling back into my head. The burst of fireworks through my body set off a storm of electric hot spasms. So much so I fall to the couch, my knees giving out.

Ryker doesn't let that stop him. He places his knees on either side of my legs and thrusts again. On the end of the orgasm, I feel another one starting. In this position, he hits my clit just perfectly with his balls. It feels tighter, like I'm clamping his cock in a new way.

"Fuck, you are so damn sexy and beautiful." I feel his hand on my ass, rubbing the little hole that has never had anything inside of it. My body jerks. "Trust me, beautiful."

At his words, I relax.

When he slowly presses his thumb inside, pain mixed with something else swirls together with the arousal between my legs. There are so many sensations all at once, mingling and ready to blow us both into oblivion.

Gripping the couch with both hands, I bury my face into it, muffling my cries, groans, and gasps. Hell, the noises coming out of me are so foreign I'm not sure they are from me.

As he presses his thumb further into my ass then wiggles it around, that movement does it. I'm slammed with the mother of all orgasms. My stomach coils, abs tighten, core clenches, and lights begin to dance behind my eyes. The pleasure races through me like water getting let out by a dam. Each sensation rushing to see who can get where the fastest.

"Fuck!" Ryker yells, then groans, "Austyn."

I feel him moving inside me, his chest hitting my back as he heaves in breaths. Wetness coats us both.

I'm pretty sure I can't move. Even with his full weight on top of me, I'm not crushed in the slightest. If anything, I feel very well-loved.

His cock still inside me twitches and jumps.

Damn, I love him so much, and it scares the ever-loving shit out of me.

CHAPTER TWENTY-THREE

RYKER

"Matthew, please tell me where they are!" my mother cries from the other end of the phone line. Personally, it's surprising it took her this long to call me. The only thing I can think is James has been up her ass and she couldn't call me. That's on her, not me.

This could also be a trap instigated by James. I wasn't born yesterday. He's deceiving on every level.

"I have no idea what you're talking about."

Austyn looks across the table at me, scooping a spoonful of Apple Jacks into her mouth, her brow raised.

I smile in return and lift my chin, telling her everything is fine.

"You know exactly what I'm talking about! You took my girls!" my mother screeches so loudly I have to pull the phone away from my ear then rub the sting out of it.

"You must have your wires crossed, Mom. I don't know anything about this."

Austyn smiles with the spoon between her lips. It shouldn't be sexy, but it is. She breathes and it's pretty much sexy.

"Mathew! They are minors! You cannot just come to my house and leave with them. You have no right to do that!"

There is so much I want to say to this. So much I want to yell at her. This is all her fault for keeping my siblings in this life. A life that is mapped out for them, where they have no choices. I get she's brainwashed, but there isn't a damn thing I can do for her unless she wants it. And that's not in the cards for her. It pisses me off.

"Like I said, I have no idea what you're talking about."

"Will you stop saying that? Yes, you do!"

Fed up, I tell her, "I have to go."

"Matth—"

I disconnect the line, not needing to hear any more of her shit. Truth is, I don't know where they are. I haven't asked Princess because it's too soon and she won't give me the information. Mostly to protect me so when questions like this come up about *do I know their whereabouts*, I can answer honestly because I don't.

Austyn reaches out and takes my hand, lacing our fingers together. It's a comfort I find I like a fuck of a lot. "I'm sorry."

"Beautiful, there is not one damn thing for you to be sorry about. My mother made her choice in how to live her life. She may have had help along the way, but it's her choice. My sisters wanted out. If they're old enough to be given a list of potential spouses, then they can make that decision."

"Ashley didn't," she throws out there.

"That was a curveball, I admit. But if she chooses to go back, if there is something to go back to, then that's on her. The way she clung

222

to Breanna, though, I'm sure she's on board with going away. Does it suck that I finally have them yet can't see them? Yeah, it does. But it is what it is. It's for their protection, and I'll do whatever the hell I have to, to keep them safe."

Her face warms. "That's what I love about you."

Getting up from the chair, I make my way over to Austyn, who stands. "What you love, huh?"

As a rosy pink comes to her cheeks, she tries to look away, but I grasp her chin lightly.

"Yeah," she finally says.

I slam my lips to hers and lift her. She wraps her legs around my waist.

Emery is in her room, so I take Austyn to hers and press her back against the door, our lips never disconnecting.

"I'm fuckin' you against the door, so you'd better be quiet or Emery will hear."

Her eyes flare, liking this as much as I do. It's always fun to have different kinks. It keeps the sex life fun.

I drop her legs. "Strip, fast."

Her smile is sexy as hell as she tears her clothes from her body. Once we have our own place, I'm going to make her walk around naked all the time so I have easy access.

I rip my shirt over my head and pull my cock out, wrapping him in latex.

She eyes me coyly as I lift her with ease, our mouths connecting. Lowering her onto my cock, she cries out, and I chuckle.

"You want Emery to hear?"

Her eyes grow wide.

"It's alright, beautiful, not like she hasn't heard before." Crashing my lips down on hers as I press her against the door, I pound into her like a jackhammer. She clenches around me, feeling the burn.

Her hips begin to swivel. Add that in with my thrusts and her angle, it only takes moments before I feel her grasp me so tightly I can barely pull out and push back in.

She cries into my mouth, and I suck it down greedily. Only then do I allow my release.

Our foreheads pressed together, we try to regain our breathing. When I think I can move, I make my way over to the bed, pulling out of her and laying her down. I remove the damn thing, strip off my jeans and boots, and climb into bed with her, holding her in my arms.

"I love you, too, beautiful. So damn much."

She wraps her arms around me, holding me.

Little do I know this could be the last time we ever hold each other like this.

CHAPTER TWENTY-FOUR

Austyn

Emery has been gone a lot lately, and I'm starting to think she's doing it on purpose so Ryker and I can have the place to ourselves. I don't like that one bit. As soon as her ass gets home, we're having words.

"I'll be out in a few," Ryker says, heading to the shower.

I immediately pull my laptop out. Sifting through the tapes, I see nothing new. Along with the money, no movement. He hasn't tried to pull anything out. At least, it's not documented that he has.

The Skype app dings. It's from Emery. I accept, and when I do, my blood runs cold as JK's face appears on the screen.

"Hello there, bitch," he spits out. I can't speak. "Meet me at my house in the basement, now! And come alone."

"I'm not stupid," I retort, finally finding my voice that is much steadier than I feel. The power this man once held over me ... well, it's still there, but I'll be damned if I let him see it.

Emery's wide, panicked eyes come on the screen briefly, and my heart lurches.

"Your little bitch of a roommate is as stupid as they come. You don't meet me, she gets exactly what was done to you."

The screen goes black as my body takes on a life of its own. I grab my gun and knife then toss on my pants. Ryker will be pissed I'm leaving without telling him, but I can't let Emery get hurt the way he did to me or at all.

I can still feel him ripping through me sometimes at night. No one deserves to have that happen to them. The fear so stark in her eyes … I need to get there *now*.

Grabbing my keys, I drive to the one place I never wanted to return to, but low and behold, life is throwing me one of its famous curveballs once again.

The house is the same stucco it was before, except now there are no people running around the place. No, it's eerily quiet.

Gun in hand, I make my way to the front steps. I have to steel myself when I open the door.

A man, one of the ones who hurt me, pops out. A smug grin comes across his face just before he lunges for me. The gun goes off, but I miss. He hits me hard across the face, sending me spinning and the gun flying out of my hand. *Shit!*

His bulky body falls on top of mine, already reaching above me for the gun. Snapping my leg up, I kick him in the shin just as I let my elbow fly, crashing into his nose.

"Fuckin' bitch!" he screams.

Lunging for the gun, he's there, both our hands on the gun. He's much stronger than me physically and there's no way I can outmaneuver him.

"What are ya gonna do now, bitch?" he bites out.

Lifting my foot, I connect it with his dick. His eyes widen, his grip loosens, and I shoot, hitting him in the chest several times. He lies there in a pool of blood. One down, and I have no clue how many more there are.

My breaths come rapidly as I press my back to the building, looking in every direction. Only then do I try to catch my breath. Everything races in my head.

My heart is having palpitations, and sweat breaks out over my skin. Holy shit, I just killed a man. Yes, a very bad man, but still.

Resting my head back against the wall, I expel a deep breath. There's more to do here. *Emery, I'm coming.*

Entering the room, the smell of dirt assaults me as I look around the space, one that haunts my memories. The large table is in the middle of the room with cuffs on the sides and bottom to strap a person down. A place where JK decided to filet me like a fucking fish.

"Aust …" Emery says, and my focus goes to her in the corner of the room.

JK stands behind her with a knife placed at her throat and hand over her mouth.

"Bitch, shut the fuck up!" he yells, taking the knife and carving it down her arm, deep enough for blood to pour out.

Emery screams.

"Stop it!" I yell at him, my gun still out.

JK's laugh is sinister. "You stupid little cunt." He drags the blade up, putting it at her throat again. "Would you rather me cut here?"

"No!"

That damn smile haunts my dreams.

The walls seem to close in on me. It takes effort to breathe in and out steadily.

I left the comfort of home with Ryker and didn't tell him where I was going. Emery is my best friend, though. I'd do anything for her in the blink of an eye. The thought of JK having her made me physically sick. No one deserves what he can dish out.

Shit. I need to get us out of here.

"I told you I'd get to you. And your little bitch of roommate is helping with that. Now I'm going to destroy you."

"Boss." I jump at a second man's voice coming through a door off to the left. "We got company." He then takes back off through the door, not even looking my way.

My heart hammers as I hold the gun steady in front of me. There is no way JK's going to get away with this. I want him dead. Not just for me, but for the fear in Emery's eyes and what he did to Deke. I thought about eliciting my revenge by cutting parts of his body off— mainly his dick—and feeding them to him, but now I don't want any of it. I just want him dead. Gone. Finished. Out of all our lives forever.

"Austyn!" Ryker's voice comes from the doorway, one of JK's assholes behind him, gun to his head. Another one who touched me. Knowing that, fury bubbles inside me. "Are you okay?"

God, how did he find me? And so quickly? I don't want him anywhere near this man, and now he has a gun to his head. I love him. Really love him. And now I've done this to him—falling for JK's words. The gun to his head is on my shoulders. *Fuck me.*

"Yeah."

"Fuck. Emery, you, too!"

"I'm okay," she says, but it comes out croaky.

I stare into her eyes. It takes her a moment, but then the fear begins to go deeper inside her and the fight begins to come out. We can fucking do this shit—three against two. True, Ryker and Emery each have weapons trained on them, but I'm not going to focus on that. Only on how the hell to get us out of here.

"Aw, isn't this just pathetically precious?" JK says as Ryker is brought further into the room. The asshole behind him kicks his knees out, making him fall hard to the floor with a *thump*.

"Fucker, you'll pay for that," Ryker growls.

JK laughs. "Nah. By the time your little friends come, we'll be finished here." His focus comes to me.

Thoughts of how I'm going to get us all out of this race through my brain. Each idea shittier than the next, considering the gun is at Ryker's temple and probably why he hasn't moved much.

"Let Emery go," I demand of JK, who's deep chuckle fills the space.

He takes the blade and places it along Emery's waist. "How far should I go in? Should I just go surface, or go really deep so she remembers me for the rest of her fucking life?" He scrapes the blade along her belly, and I'm thankful of the shirt taking the brunt of the cut. It's in shreds, but who cares? It hasn't cut into her belly yet.

"Stop! What do you want?"

JK's eyes come back to mine. "For you to fucking die!"

From the way he holds Emery, I can't get a good shot, so I take a step to the right. He counters it, then pushes the blade into her flesh, making blood ooze out. I still.

"Please don't do this!" Emery cries out.

JK's eyes still on mine, he asks Ryker, "Your little whore's pussy is delectable, isn't it? You know, it was the luck of the draw that I got the little Ravage MC princess in my hunt that night."

Bile rises from my stomach, burning my throat as I force it down.

"Shut up!" I scream, the gun wavering as tears form in the corner of my eyes. I try to stand strong, but his words are cutting me to the quick.

JK's smile widens. "Oh, you mean your little boy toy here doesn't know that you murdered *my* baby?"

"I'm sorry," I say softly to Ryker, who says nothing, though his eyes turn cold.

Fear slams into me hard.

Emery whimpers in the background.

"That virgin pussy was enough, but then you had to go and kill my baby!" JK screams. "For that, bitch, you will die!" With the knife now at Emery's throat, he begins to dig in and dig deep.

The gun is steady in my hand, the weight of it not giving me a bit of comfort. The cold of the metal, the unforgiveness of its mold, it matches the way I feel inside. Hardened steel, molded and made by the hands of men, the firearm gives me no fear. It only feeds the burning need for retribution in my soul.

Aiming it at him, thoughts of how I got to this place rush through me. The choices that were stripped, the consequences of actions and life that were altered and changed forever. All of it weighs heavily on me, but my strong shoulders bear it.

Being a warrior is in my blood, carried through me from my parents. Eye for an eye is our motto. They would expect nothing less from me.

The blood pumping through my veins was once a life source. Now, my sole focus and the fury that courses through me is fueled by vengeance with every beat of my heart.

Ryker looks up at me, eyes blank.

"Bye, Ryker."

I eye Emery, darting them to the left quickly. Even with tears streaming down her face, she catches it, moving fast as she lunges. I take that as my opportunity.

Without a second thought or a moment of hesitation, I pull the trigger, sending off several rounds into JK's chest. He jerks back, the arm with the knife flying upward. Then JK's body falls to the ground with a hard *thump*.

The gurgling sounds coming from him make my stomach roll. Blood seeps from his lips, pooling on the floor as he turns on his side and begins to cough. For good measure, I put a bullet in his head, thanking my mother for her target practices. When he stops moving, I turn my attention to the rest of the room.

Ryker is moving fast, subduing the man behind him. He rips the gun from him and pulls the trigger.

As blood squirts from the guy's neck, the man reaches up, trying to stop the flow, his eyes wide with fear. He collapses on the ground, and then Ryker steps forward and puts a few more shots into him until the man stills.

This is all surreal. I want to cry and curl into a ball. I want to disappear into nothing. Instead, I rush toward Emery, whose hand is at her neck, trying to stop the blood flow.

"Is it deep?"

"Part of it is."

Fuck!

I pull off my shirt and place the fabric against her neck. "Put pressure on it."

Ryker sweeps Emery up into his arms then grabs my arm. "We need to get the fuck out of here. I took out one of the guys before that asshole found me. I don't know how many more are here. The guys are about five out."

Sucking in much-needed air, I follow him and Emery through the room. We pass by JK, who now lies in a pool of blood, his eyes looking straight up, sending a shiver down my spine.

He's gone. Officially gone. Too bad it wasn't soon enough.

Gun fire can be heard from outside.

Ryker sticks his head out. "They're here."

Relief washes over me for only a moment.

It's all over. All of it.

JK.

Ryker and me.

He knows now. The dirt and grime. He knows all of it, and I don't feel one bit relieved.

It's all over.

Everything.

CHAPTER TWENTY-FIVE

RYKER

Virgin pussy? My baby? Fucking hell.

Austyn gave her virginity to a man like JK? That doesn't make sense. Even if she didn't know who he was, she's not that kind of woman. She has to care about someone to get to that level. It took her how long to finally let me in, and I'm supposed to believe she gave herself to JK?

Austyn lies curled up in a ball on the bed in my room at the clubhouse. I haven't been here in a long-ass time and the room smells like it, but Austyn says nothing.

Emery is patched up and physically fine. Emotionally is another story, but Angel and GT are taking care of her. Austyn wouldn't leave Emery's side until GT finally told her that she needed to go lie down and he had Emery.

As I sit on the bed next to her, her body jolts. Reaching out, I caress her hip as she begins to cry. With her knees against her chest, I form myself to her body as she starts to shake.

We don't talk. We simply lie there while she cries.

It takes hours before she calms enough for me to speak, and I hate to even ask this, but I need to know more about what he said.

"It was his baby?"

When she begins to sob again, I hold her tighter.

"Yeah …"

"Why? Why would you have sex with a man like that?"

Her body stops shaking and begins to vibrate. "You think I *let* him? No, I didn't let him, Ryker."

Anger heats me from the inside out, boiling like hot lava out of a volcano. She didn't *let* him. Let him. He took it.

"Please tell me what happened." My voice is so low. I don't trust myself not to scare the shit out of her with the fury I feel.

"I don't want to." She shakes her head into the pillow.

"It's already out now, Austyn. Release yourself from all of it."

She cries more, and I hate it, but I need to know what happened. If she didn't give herself freely, that's the underlying reason she pulled away from me. Why she thinks she dirty. Why she's been through hell longer than anyone, including myself, realized. It makes sense now, and I fucking hate it. She needs to say the words, get it out there and in the open.

Her entire body shudders, almost as if she's having a seizure, as prickles form on her skin. I wrap her tighter in my warmth and wait.

"You don't want to hear this," she says softly between her broken cries. "You don't want this vision in your head, Ryker. It'll change everything."

Kissing the top of her head, I promise her, "Nothing changes. Not one damn thing between you and I. Swear it."

Austyn takes her time, probably sorting out in her head how she wants to tell me this, knowing it's under protest, just like the last time. But JK already spilled it. She needs to wash herself clean of it once and for all.

"I met Jill in Spear at Club Cam's. She's an old friend, or I thought she was, from school. She wanted to go out and let loose. I was fine with that. I didn't have much to do and Emery was away at school. So, I went. We drank and danced. She ended up going home with a guy, totally ditching me. I went out front and called a cab to come get me."

She begins to shake, and I give her a reassuring squeeze. Then she blows out a deep breath.

"While I was waiting, JK approached me, asking me for a cigarette. We ended up striking a conversation. This is where it gets a little hazy.

"I was poked with something sharp, and my entire body felt … different. So different. He led me to a car, but I can't remember if I protested. Then he took off and I closed my eyes because I felt nauseous. When I came to, I was strapped to a bed."

My body begins to tremble. Locking it down proves difficult. Heat fills me like a fire with too much gasoline on it, expanding out of control. It's like one of those wildfires that's so intense it's hard to control. For Austyn's sake, though I do, at least on the outside.

"They hit me, hurt me. JK was first …" She hiccups as I try to absorb her pain. "They took turns with me." Austyn burrows her face into the pillow, trying to pull away from me, but I don't let her get far.

"Austyn, none of that shit was your fault."

"I know." Her voice breaks. "But it makes me dirty."

Turning her in my arms, I find her entire face is red with splotches, wetness coats her cheeks, and her eyes are puffy red. Pain is everywhere. In her eyes, posture, and her soul.

"You are not dirty. Not one fuckin' thing about you is dirty."

"I can't get clean," she whispers, her eyes calling to me, tugging at my heart.

Rubbing her arm up and down, I tell her, "You are clean. What they did to you is on them. It makes them dirty, sick fuckers. It makes them unworthy to breathe air. You, you're not any of that. It wasn't your choice. They did those things to you without your consent. Nothing about this is dirty for you."

Everything inside me aches for Austyn. It's as if, with each word, she's yanking out pieces of her heart and soul and throwing them on the ground. Then I come along and pick them up, putting them back where they need to go.

She's broken and cracked from what those men did to her. It makes me want to kill the fucker myself and add in some serious pain. She did that, though. She took care of the problem, making it so he's no longer a threat.

"I want to believe that, Ryker. It's why I didn't want to tell you." She shakes her head as more tears stream down her face and onto the pillow below.

I cup the side of her face, brushing some hair away from her eyes. "I understand, but babe, I'm all in with you. The good, the bad, and the ugly. Whatever life slams us in the face with, I'm by your side. But I fuckin' swear to you, nothing like this will ever happen to you again. I'll protect you until my dyin' breath."

She grips me hard, pressing her face into my chest as her body racks with sobs once again.

"How'd you get away?" I ask softly, wanting the rest of the story, but not wanting to upset her even more.

"That's the thing; after he looked in my wallet and got my name, he threatened me, saying he would come back and do it again if I opened my mouth. Then he said something about the younger girls in Ravage, which I would never let happen. Then he just pushed me into a car, and the next thing I remember, I was in my car, sitting in the parking lot at the bar."

That fucking dickhead did so much more damage than any of us thought. He tore this woman to shreds, but he will not win. The Austyn I've been with the past few weeks is the woman she's meant to be— happy, loved, and laughing.

That's where we'll get back to. I fuckin' swear it.

CHAPTER TWENTY-SIX

Austyn

I didn't think a human could cry so many tears. There should be no more water inside my body, considering it's all over Ryker and the bed below us.

His warmth surrounds me, allowing me to feel safe and protected. This man, whom I've loved for so damn long, sees past all the shit I just laid out on him and told me he was *all in*.

That's all I have. There are no more secrets. There is no more holding back. It's all released and floating off my shoulders into thin air. He knows the secrets I've been trying to hold close to me, and even though he's heard it, he still wants to be with me.

Maybe he's right and I'm not as dirty as I thought. Or, is this just a Band-Aid covering up the grime? I wish I knew the answer.

There is nothing now holding me back from loving Ryker the way he deserves. There is nothing restricting how I act or feel toward him.

There is nothing but him and me, and that's all that matters. I feel it in my soul. He is my soul; has been for years. He's just confirmed I'm his.

My mother always told me that when *the one* came, it would hit me hard and fast. What she didn't tell me is the journey I'd have to go on to find my happiness. After all this clears and the pain of it all dissipates, I hope my happiness with Ryker will be staring me in the face.

I have a feeling it will.

"Do you want the club to know?" Ryker breaks the peaceful silence, knocking the wind out of me.

My body trembles as the panic sets in. "I ..."

I feel Ryker's fingertips under my chin. He lifts it so our gazes connect. "You don't want to, that's fine. My lips are sealed until my dyin' breath. But beautiful, you get this all out in the open, there's nothin' holdin' you back. There's no question if anyone ever finds out later in life and it blows up, openin' old wounds. It's done and over with, and you can move past it all."

More fucking tears. Everything inside me coils up like a spring ready to snap at any given moment. I rub my feet together rhythmically, wanting to get up and walk, while I fight the urge to stick my thumb in my mouth.

He's right in some ways, but wrong in others. The weight that lifted when Ryker accepted me for who I am is priceless. On the other hand, people may see me as the dirty girl I thought myself to be for so long. The pity will come back, and I don't know if I can deal with that.

He's also right that, if everyone knows, then nothing can be held over my head later in life. The Ravage MC have enemies, and there will always be that little inkling that it will open wide once again at any moment.

"I don't know what to do," I tell him honestly. Both ways have their positives.

"Listen to your gut, beautiful. Ravage is your family, and you know we protect our own. Will it be a shock? Fuck yeah. Will people be pissed as hell? Fuck yeah. Will people want to kill that fucker again for what he did to you? Fuck yeah to that, too. Will they look down on you or think less of you? Fuck no. They will not see any dirt on you. They will only be there to hold you up."

Fear grips me in its hold, threatening to suck the life out of me. This is so much for one person to handle.

I remember how blindsided I felt when Deke pulled me into the room with my father and Ryker, like a two-by-four slammed into my head. It wasn't on my terms. It was on theirs. I can't have that again. It needs to be on mine so I'm not smacked again with this years down the road.

I don't know if anyone will ever find out, but I also thought I could keep my pregnancy a secret and that blew up in my face.

The thing is, as much as I don't want to stand in front of my family and tell them, I have to be the one to do it. Strength isn't measured in how much you can bench press. It's measured in your actions. This will be my action. The last one for this, and then it will all be closed. I can shut the door on this part of my life and move on.

It won't be easy, but life isn't meant to be easy. It's meant to challenge you and guide you. Shitty things happen to people, but it's how you overcome them and stand on your own two feet that matters in the end.

"Okay. I want this over with."

Ryker pulls me to his lips. The touch is light but reassuring. "Then we move on from this. You and me."

"Yeah."

Initially, I wanted to do this at my mother's house, thinking it would be more intimate and warm. After thinking about it long and hard, though, I didn't want to taint my parents' home with it. Therefore, Ryker set it up for everyone to be at the clubhouse.

Laughter rings out through the room with bottles tapping on tables. My mother isn't doing any of that. Her gaze is completely on me, reaching into my brain and pulling out whatever it is she wants to know. Weird how moms can do that.

The children are all downstairs, and I bet if Mazie got her way, they are watching that pirate movie again.

Ryker's arm is around my waist as I drum up the courage to speak. Sweat breaks out over my skin, and I thank God I put on extra deodorant today. Butterflies swarm in my belly, and bile threatens to escape my mouth. My thumb goes to said mouth as I begin to chew.

A hand comes up, and Ryker pulls my thumb away from my mouth. He clasps his hand with mine, intertwining our fingers. "Ready?"

I shake my head, and as I do, my mother becomes alert, even more so than before.

"Yes, you are. Let's do this and be done."

Letting out a deep breath, I squeeze his hand. "Okay."

Ryker lets out a piercing whistle, catching everyone's attention. The room quiets.

"Austyn has something she wants to tell ya. Not a fuckin' word from anyone," Ryker warns, causing a smile to tip my lips. Damn, I love this man.

As all eyes fall on me, my pulse picks up, my heart threatening to jump from my chest and run a marathon.

Ryker pulls me into his side and kisses the top of my head reassuringly.

Letting out a deep breath, I begin, "You all know I was pregnant." My eyes veer over to Deke, who has Riley sitting next to him, holding her hand, with Emery on his other. His focus is on me.

Emery gives me a small smile. The bandages on her arm and neck freeze me in place for a moment. It pisses me off that he touched her, but it could've been a lot worse. I'm thankful it wasn't.

Sucking in a deep breath, I focus.

"I'm just going to blurt this out and get it done with. JK was the father of the baby."

Gasps and wide eyes are seen throughout the room, making my stomach twist into a knot.

I hurry and continue, "He drugged me outside of Club Cam's and took me to a place—I don't know where. He and his three friends took turns with … me."

The sound of several chairs screeching across the floor then falling with loud clashes get me to open my eyes that I didn't realize I'd closed. My father, Deke, Cooper, and Nox are all up on their feet, their focus solely on me, fury radiating off them like no other.

"It's done. He's dead. But … Ryker and I talked about it and thought it was best for everyone to know. I didn't tell you to be pissed off, but I wanted you to know so this will never come up again. I want this laid to rest and in the past. I don't want anyone talking about it or feeling sorry for me in any way. I don't need pity. I just want everyone to know so it will never get held over me or any of you in the future."

Letting out a deep breath, Ryker pulls me to his side, kissing my temple.

"You fuckin' shittin' me!" This, surprisingly, comes from Deke. "This is because of *me*. All this fuckin' shit!" he yells, flipping the table in front of him as Rylie screams out.

Only then do I break away from Ryker and walk up to Deke. Ryker tries to pull me back, noting the blazing red fury coming from Deke, but I know he'd never hurt me.

Deke heaves in and out, his fists clenched at his sides. His intense gaze hits me like a brand, but that doesn't stop me from talking.

"He didn't know who I was until after it was all over." Deke's nostrils flare. "He only found out because he looked through my purse and found my driver's license. You had nothing to do with this, Deke. It was the wrong place, wrong time."

"You lyin' to make me calm down?"

I shake my head vehemently. "I lied to you once and vowed I'd never do it again, Deke. It's the truth."

Deke reaches out and pulls me to his chest, wrapping me up. "I'm so fuckin' sorry," he says in my ear.

"Not your fault, Deke."

He squeezes me tighter, and that's how I spend the afternoon.

All wrapped up in my family.

CHAPTER TWENTY-SEVEN

RYKER

"Church," Cruz calls out, which is to be expected after Austyn just dropped the bomb. In all honesty, they took it better than I thought. I mean, hell, only one flipped table; that's pretty damn good for the club.

I eye my woman from across the room. She's sitting with Emery and her mother. When I catch her eye, I lift my chin. She gives me a smile in recognition.

Making my way into church, I feel all their eyes scanning me, searching for answers. This should be fun.

Cruz calls attention. "What else do you know? And is that the reason you had Breaker take pictures of those assholes and send them to you?"

I lean back in my chair on a sigh. "That's all I know. Everything is out in the open. As for the pictures, I showed them to Austyn so she could identify all four of the assholes who touched her. Fuck, she killed two of them herself."

Cruz runs his hands through his hair, pain searing his expression. He loves his girl. There hasn't been one time I saw him with her when he didn't have his arm around her or laughing with her. Cruz is one scary motherfucker, but his wife and kids are his world. This is tearing him up.

"You're fuckin' sure all those assholes are dead?" Cooper asks from next to his father, while Deke stares at me, waiting for the answer.

"She ID'd them clear out. Even trembled when she did so. It's them. This shit is over with, and Austyn wants it laid to rest. That's why she told you. She doesn't want this shit hanging over her head. It's done. Over."

"Fuck, I want to crush that motherfucker." Deke clenches and unclenches his fists on top of the table. There's no doubt he's feeling like his retribution didn't get finished. JK fucked with his life by getting him addicted to drugs then threatening the kids of the Ravage MC if he didn't leave. When Deke did leave, it caused a horrible rift between him and his father. Deke wanted to be the one to put the bullet in JK. I can't blame him.

"Know that, but Austyn got there first, even if I want to fuckin' strangle her for it."

Deke's brows go up, as does Cooper's. Cooper is the one to speak.

"So, you've been attached to her fuckin' hip for the last, hell, I don't even know how long, and you let her slip through?"

I knew this was coming.

Rubbing my hands over my face, I say, "Got out of the shower and heard the door shut. Lucky for me, it took her a minute, fumbling with her keys to get the door locked. I got dressed, let her get in her car, and followed her. Called you guys, and the rest, you know."

"I'm just fuckin' glad the asshole's gone," Cooper says.

"Not fuckin' me," Rhys puts in. "I could've had a hell of a fun time with him." He pulls out his knife and runs the blade over his fingertips.

"No shit," Cruz says, slapping his hands down on the table. "Is she okay?"

Inhaling deeply, I let it out. "No, but she will be. It's a rush for all this to come out. Brother, she was going to keep it to the grave, and if JK hadn't said anything about it bein' his baby, I would've never picked it up. But it's over. We all know everything, and it's done with. Let's move the fuck on and don't look back."

"Right, so you're off duty and need to be back at the shop," GT cuts in. "It also means you can move out of my niece's place."

I flex my fingers. "Right, like that's gonna happen."

"Right," Cruz says, standing up and holding the gavel. "Better not hurt her or I'll rip your heart out and feed it to the wolves." The gavel slams down in finality.

I have no doubt what he says is true. Good thing I don't ever intend on hurting my woman.

"Now go get her. We have to all talk to her about what she did."

I've been dreading this for a while now, knowing it was coming. She hacked into Ravage's computers, which is something that isn't done. Might as well get all this shit done in one go.

"I'll be back."

I move out in search of my woman, knowing that, no matter what happens in that room, I'll protect her. I find her sitting at a bunch of tables with her mother and some of the other ol' ladies, including Emery.

She smiles as I approach, but it falls when she sees the look on my face. I'm not sure what it is, but she's hesitant about it.

"They want to talk to ya."

Panic flashes in her eyes, but she quickly masks it and rises.

Princess stares at us. I just lift my chin, letting her know I'll take care of my girl.

Out of earshot, I tell Austyn, "They know you hacked into the Ravage computers. I actually knew a long time ago, but we were letting you ride."

She gasps, pulling away from me, eyes as wide as saucers.

"You're gonna go in there with your head held high and deal with whatever is said."

She clasps her throat. "I'm in trouble?" she whispers.

"Not as much as you'd think, but yeah. They want to talk to you."

We make it to the door.

"As much as I've been in this room, I should just be a patched member." She gives a little chuckle, letting me know she's okay. She may be a little scared, but she's going to be alright.

I knock once then enter. Everyone turns their heads as I lead Austyn to the front.

Cruz rises and wraps his arms around her, kissing her on the head.

"Looks like I'm in the principal's office again," she jokes, and the room chuckles. That's better than how I thought this would be. Ravage doesn't take this shit lightly. She knows this just as well as I do.

The air in the room turns serious as I take my seat, my eyes glued to my woman. She looks nervous but is holding herself together, not even biting her thumb. I'm impressed. However, my thoughts are up in the air on how this could go.

"Tell me," Cruz says as he sits back in his chair.

Having Austyn on display in front of everyone is a tactic we often use in interrogation.

"The night of one of the parties, I went into Buzz's room and saved all the information you had on JK onto my flash drive. I took it home and looked through it all." She breathes out her words, almost coming out as a long paragraph without any breaks.

"So, you stole from Ravage," GT, the vice president and her uncle, says.

Her eyes shift. "I thought of it as sharing information."

Buzz clears his throat. "You know that shit is encrypted with so many obstacles that no human or other computer should be able to get into it."

"Um …"

Buzz continues, "And you were able to do it and put shit back to a point I had to really search to find out what exactly you took and when."

This time, she says nothing.

"And you picked my fuckin' lock."

Austyn closes her eyes then opens them, clasping her hands in front of her. "I'm sorry. I needed to find JK before any of you did. I wanted my revenge, and I wanted him to stay quiet about everything that happened. I didn't think of it as stealing from any of you. I'm sorry if you do. I was blinded by vengeance." She blows out a breath, her hair going up with it then back down to her face.

"What do you think we should do about it?" Cruz asks conversationally. If this were anyone else for any other reason, he'd be in a face-off with them, no questions asked.

"You can have the money. It's millions, Dad. It's all JK's. I rerouted it to an account I set up. It should be there by now. I'll wire it to

Ravage."

"The money you hopped around went into an account for you?" Buzz asks.

Austyn nods while I lean back in my chair. I guess there was another secret I didn't know about.

"It was payback for what he did to me. I thought I could donate some of it, and then live comfortably on the rest. But I did wrong, and as my penance, I'll wire all the money to Ravage's accounts."

Cruz looks around the room. Austyn has been here her whole life. Been through more than any woman deserves. Still, I know they can't fully let it go. There has to be some consequences or it will happen again, and that can't happen.

"Half. Half the money dumped into Ravage's accounts. Buzz will help you with it."

Austyn nods, looking down at her hands.

"The rest of it, you start over—fresh. That fucker has no more pull on you. No touch. He doesn't exist. Understood?"

"Yes," she replies.

"Since that's done," Buzz says, slamming his hand on the table, "you and me are gonna have some sessions in front of the computer, because you're going to show me how you did everything so I can make the system stronger."

"Of course. But Tug's the one who taught me the locks."

"Pft!" Buzz chimes out, looking over at Tug. "That shit's child's play. Computers are the answer."

"Fucker," Tug says on a laugh, and it's done.

Cruz gets up and hugs his daughter, along with everyone else in the room. When she gets to me, I don't let her go. Even when she transferred the money over and talked to Buzz, she did it on my lap.

CHAPTER TWENTY-EIGHT

Austyn

"Mom, seriously, I said we were coming and I mean it." Rolling my eyes up to the ceiling does nothing to hide the irritation in my words. Even through the phone, I know my mother can sense it.

"You better be. This is family day."

"I know. I'm not going to hide out like I did before. Everything is good."

"No, you'll just hide out in your place with your man. Don't think I don't know you didn't come to the party last weekend because you were curled up with him."

I chuckle because she's right. "Yep, and if you were me, you would've done the same."

"You're probably right, but don't miss today." There's a smile in her voice.

"Be there in a bit."

"Good." She disconnects as Ryker wraps his arms around me. I let my head fall back to his shoulder.

"It's not a bad idea, ya know—getting back in bed and letting me fuck you until tomorrow," he says in my ear then gives it a nibble.

I let out a chuckle that turns into a moan. "Yeah, but my mother will probably be here to rip your balls off."

"Ouch. Way to kill the mood."

"Emery!" I yell out just as she comes out of her room. Dressed in jeans and a tank, she's beautiful like always. Damn, I'd kill for that hair.

"Shut it, woman. I'm here." She stuffs something into her bag. "Let's go."

We take Ryker's bike, and Emery follows in her car.

People surround the clubhouse. As I get off the bike, I feel like I'm home. Food is consumed, along with laughter and a ton of beer.

Bristyl comes over and grabs my hands. "You need anything ever, you talk to me," she says with a smile.

"Thanks."

Rylynn breaks away from her mother, Tanner and comes over to greet us. We haven't seen her in a long time. One, because Rhys has her under lock and key when she's here; and two, she's away at school. She just finished her freshman year of college, and I'm so damn happy to have her home. We aren't as close as Emery and I are, but we're still family.

She falls into my arms, wrapping hers around me. "I love you. Anything you want to talk about, I'm here. No questions asked."

With a wide smile on my face, I pull back. "Thanks, but I'm good. How about you?"

Something flashes in her eyes. "School sucks, but whatever."

"Sorry."

She waves her hand in the air. "Pft. No worries. I'll make it, always do."

We sit and chat for what feels like forever.

That's when the air in the room changes.

Micah, Tug and Blaze's son, comes strolling into the clubhouse. A clubhouse, mind you, that he has wanted nothing to do with for years.

When he was younger, he always had his head in a video game, saying he wanted nothing to do with the club. He made it his point—no, his mission—that everyone know he'd never be part of the club.

Emery has loved that boy since they were little, but he has never once given her the time of day. Never. It's like she doesn't even exist to him. He's a fucking moron if you ask me.

What the real kicker is, he has a gorgeous, leggy woman on his arm, with long, thick blonde hair down her back and sparkling blue eyes.

I have to blink a couple times because I could have sworn it was Emery on his arm, but no, it's almost an exact replica of her. Almost. *Holy fuck.*

Darting my eyes around the room, they land on Emery, whose jaw is dropped as she takes in Micah. I'm not going to lie, he looks damn good with his dark hair and five o'clock shadow. But fuck, this is going to cut Emery to the quick. There's no way to stop it.

As Micah begins to make his rounds, Emery becomes unstuck.

I move away from Ryker, who came over to talk with Rylynn and me. "Gotta get the tequila."

He chuckles as I move to the bar and ask the prospect for a bottle and two shot glasses.

Emery slides up to me, not saying a word.

"Looks like we have a date with Jose tonight," I tell her, sliding a glass in front of her.

She doesn't hesitate, slamming it in one glug then tapping the glass back on the bar.

"We have a long fuckin' date with Jose, Austyn. Long fuckin' date."

Tequila is poured, and we drink ... a lot. Rylynn comes over and has a couple of shots. She may only be nineteen, but she's with family.

A few hours later, Micah and his Emery clone come up to us. And I'm pretty happy that Emery is three sheets to the wind or this could be really bad. Or maybe her being three sheets is bad. *Shit.*

"Hey, Austyn, Emery. How's it goin'?" he asks as Emery takes another shot. I've lost count of what we're on, but Ryker hasn't come over to intervene, so I guess we're not totally lost yet.

"Good. You?" I answer for her.

"Good. This is Jacklyn," Micah introduces.

I give a small wave as Emery's lips tip up just a bit in a snarl, then she releases it.

"Hi," Emery finally says. I can see her jaw clenched, fighting back from saying any more.

"How are you doing, Emery?" he asks, still holding the girl next to him.

She looks up to the ceiling. "A knife to the neck, arm, and stomach ... Doin' peachy. You?"

Micah looks stunned for a moment. That's when I see Jacks, one of the brothers, out of the corner of my eye. He's one of the quiet ones, always in the background, but never really far away. He strolls up to Emery, putting his arm around her and pulling her gently to his side.

He looks at Micah. "Glad I got the real one," he says then takes off.

Micah gapes, and I laugh my ass off. He doesn't know what he's missing. *Dumbass.*

In this moment, I would buy Jacks anything he wants. The look on Micah's face is priceless.

Curled up in bed with my man with me is the best way to end the night. Well, it's much better than praying to the porcelain gods, which I'm surprised hasn't happened. I think it's because, after the Micah incident, Ryker took the bottle away. Then I had the chance to let it permeate through my body. It'll either be a blessing when I wake up, or I'll have a killer hangover.

Right now, I don't care.

Drawing small circles on his chest with my fingernails, I watch as his skin jumps when I hit certain spots. I make it my mission to hit those more often.

I love that I have that effect on him. I love that he's the one lying next to me, loving me the way I always dreamed.

Shit happens in life. Sometimes we're dealt a hand that's hard to bear. Then sometimes you're blessed with something you never imagined possible. It's those times you have to hold on to. Have to care for and nurture. I've learned they are the best moments in life.

"You're thinkin' awfully hard there," Ryker says from above me. I move my head so I can see his gorgeous face.

"Thank you."

Puzzlement fills his face. "For ...?"

"Loving me. Accepting me and giving me everything I've ever dreamed of."

A sexy grin tips his lips. "Beautiful, loving you is how I breathe. That'll never change."

My heart melts as his head comes down, kissing me senseless.

EPILOGUE

RYKER

Leaning against my truck outside the sperm donor's main offices, I watch as people rush in and out of the buildings. I'm not one to help the government out or anything, but it was necessary this time. Watching all the officers going in and out with boxes and computers only makes me smile.

Buzz found shit I didn't even know existed. All of it damning. But the one that got me were records from the children. One of the mothers was only fifteen-years-old. Therefore, my sperm donor will not only be seeing the inside of a cell for money laundering, tax evasion, and other money-related things, he'll also be spending time for statutory rape of a minor. Not only him, but William is also facing those charges.

There are enough men in the same boat as my sperm donor that it should completely dismantle this operation. Including the fact that the Feds froze all their money.

My mother hasn't spoken to me, but I have a feeling she'll come around once all her funds have disappeared. It's only a matter of time. Maybe I'll be able to see my younger siblings soon.

Samantha has never called back.

Breanna and Ashley called me the other night, surprising the shit out of me. My first thought was that something was wrong, since they were told not to call on unless it was an emergency. It wasn't.

They are adjusting very well with Xavier and Kim. Breanna says it was really hard for her at first, but as time went on, she was able to come to terms that she wouldn't be able to talk to her mother. I didn't tell her about what was going on, figuring that she'll hear it on the news if it makes it that far.

Who knows, maybe my mother can get her head out of her ass and see them again, without all the other bullshit.

Arms and ankles crossed, ass leaning against the truck, I wait.

When my sperm donor comes out, his hands in shackles behind him, I smile inside.

His eyes come up to mine and turn furious. All I do is lift my chin and get in the truck. He needs to know all this was because of me. He needs to know that he can't touch me anymore. He needs to know that his time as king is done and over with. He's finished. It's the ultimate revenge. The biggest kind of "fuck you" I dish out without putting him six feet under.

I drive back to Austyn's apartment and enter without knocking, just like I always do. While I love that she has her own place, I'm tired of living like this. So, I have a surprise for her.

"Hey, baby. Work was crazy. My feet are killing me today," she tells me with a smile. She loves her job, and I'm happy she's found something she enjoys. Not that she has to work, but it makes her happy.

That's all that matters.

"I want you to close your eyes." I grab a scarf and put it around her eyes. "We're going somewhere, and I want you to not look until we get there."

"Okay. I trust you, Ryker." Those words are almost as good as when she tells me she loves me.

We get on the bike, and then I wrap her arms around me. "Hold on."

The drive isn't long. I didn't want to be too far away from the clubhouse. Our family is there.

I pull up and cut the bike. Then, reaching back, I help her off.

"What is it, Ryker?"

Stepping behind her, my hands on her shoulders, I tell her, "Love stayin' with you at your place, but remember when I told you I was all in?"

She nods as I pull away the scarf.

"I meant I was *all in*."

She gasps, putting her hand over her mouth, eyes wide. "Oh, my God."

"Do you like it?"

The house is gorgeous. It sits off to the side of a little lake on a few acres. The house needed some work, but my brothers helped get it ready. It's a ranch-style with three bedrooms and two baths, with a huge wraparound porch. It even has a sitting room that faces the sun. It's perfect.

"Love it? This is ours?"

I hold out the keys to her. "I'm all in, beautiful. It's ours."

She leans up and kisses me. "I'm all in, too, Ryker. Love you."

261

"Love you too."

A grim look comes over her face. "I can't leave Emery. This is great, and I can't wait to have our own place, but I can't leave her alone. I know she's been spending a lot of time with Jacks, but I can't not be there when she gets back."

Emery has had a few nightmares about being held at knife point, and I say few, but Austyn is an overprotective mother hen. I knew that going into this endeavor.

I lift my hand, pointing my index finger.

She stops and follows the direction I'm pointing then gasps. "What's that?"

"That's Emery's place. It's close, yet we have our own space." Emery's great, but I need my woman alone more than just in the bedroom and on the occasions Emery's not at home.

"It's beautiful." She reaches around and grabs her neck.

Austyn is looking at a smaller replica of the bigger house. It's another ranch-style, one bedroom, kitchen, and bath. It's not the Ritz, but it's kickass.

"Deke took extra time putting it together and fixing it up. The asshole even put his own money into it, not taking a dime from me."

She leans up and our lips attach while she cups my face. "Thank you. This is the best thing you could've given me."

"Nah, the best is when we christen the house."

Just then, bikes rumble and turn into the lane. All my brothers with their ol' ladies on their backs show up. Emery smiles from on the back of Jacks'.

"She knows, doesn't she?" Austyn questions.

"Yep. Already told her."

"And she never said a word!" Her hands go to her hips as she stares at Emery, who gives a little shrug.

"Come on, baby; we ride."

She smiles up at me, rolls up onto her tiptoes, and brushes a kiss against my lips. "Thank you."

"The house is all part of ..."

She brushes her lips against mine again. "No, for not giving up on me. For not letting me push you away. For being the man at my side and at my back. For loving me."

"Beautiful, I do love you." I lean down and take her lips.

Honking and the revving of bikes goes on around us, so we break away on a chuckle.

"Let's ride with our family."

"Forever."

"Damn straight. All in." She gives me a soft smile, and then we ride.

ACKNOWLEDGEMENTS

Thank you to everyone who's supported me over the years. You mean the world to me.

Thank you to my team. You're the best and I wouldn't be here without you.

ABOUT RYAN

Ryan Michele found her passion in bringing fictional characters to life. She loves being in an imaginary world where anything is possible, and she has a knack for special twists readers don't see coming.

She writes MC, Contemporary, Erotic, Paranormal, New Adult, Inspirational, and other romance-based genres. Whether it's bikers, wolf-shifters, mafia, etc., Ryan spends her time making sure her heroes are strong and her heroines match them at every turn.

When she isn't writing, Ryan is a mom and wife, living in rural Illinois and reading by her pond in the warm sun.

Ryan can be found:

Website: www.authorryanmichele.net
Facebook: www.facebook.com/AuthorRyanMichele
Instagram: @authorryanmichele
Twitter: www.twitter.com/Ryan_Michele
Goodreads: http://www.goodreads.com/RyanMichele
Email: ryanmicheleauthor@gmail.com

Other Books by Ryan

Ravage MC Series:

Ravage Me

Seduce Me

Consume Me

Inflame Me

Captivate Me

Ravage MC Novella Collection

Ride with Me (co-written with Chelsea Camaron)

Ravage MC Bound Series:

Bound by Family

Bound by Desire

Bound by Vengeance (Coming Soon)

Vipers Creed MC Series:

Challenged

Conquering

Conflicted (Coming soon)

Ruthless Rebels MC Series (co-written with Chelsea Camaron):

Shamed

Scorned

Scarred

Schooled (Coming Soon)

Loyalties Series:

Blood & Loyalties: A Mafia Romance

Raber Wolf Pack Series

Raber Wolf Pack Book 1

Raber Wolf Pack Book 2

Raber Wolf Pack Book 3

Standalone Romances

Full Length Novels:

Needing to Fall

Safe

Wanting You

Short Stories:

Hate to Love

Branded

Novellas:

Billionaire Up Romance

Stood Up

THANK YOU!

♥ Ryan
Michele

Made in the USA
Lexington, KY
26 May 2018